In addition to being a popular and prolific writer for children, Alan Gibbons teaches in a primary school. He also much in demand as a speaker in schools and at book events. He lives in Liverpool with his wife and four children.

Alan Gibbons won the Blue Peter Book Award in the 'Book I Couldn't Put Down' category for *Shadow of the Minotaur*, which was also shortlisted for the Carnegie Medal.

The Edge

ALAN GIBBONS

A Dolphin
Paperback

First published in Great Britain in 2002
as a Dolphin Paperback
by Orion Children's Books
a division of the Orion Publishing Group Ltd
Orion House
5 Upper St Martin's Lane
London WC2H 9EA

Reprinted 2002 (twice), 2003

A catalogue record for this book is
available from the British Library

Typeset at The Spartan Press Ltd,
Lymington, Hants
Printed in Great Britain by
Clays Ltd, St Ives plc

ISBN 1 84255 094 2

1

Danny

He awakes with a start. Somebody is shaking him. Roughly.

'What . . . ?'

A hand covers his mouth, choking off the question. For a moment he gives in to a surge of panic, then he makes out a face in the darkness. His mother. She is crouching by his bed, one hand on the headboard, one clamped to the lower half of his face. He can see her properly now, her features slightly illuminated by the streetlamp a couple of doors away. It's her eyes he notices first, the frightened, pleading expression. Oh no, don't tell me it's happening again. He has learned to read his mother's face. Interpreting her looks, her mouthed warnings, has been essential to his survival. But this he can't read. It is too sudden, too unexpected. He gives a questioning frown.

'We've got to go,' Mum hisses. 'Now.'

'Go? Go where?'

Her hands are waving, palms down, reinforcing the pleading look in her eyes. 'Keep your voice down, Danny,' she whispers, 'Please!'

He does as he's told. His next words are barely audible. 'What's going on?'

'Can't explain. But we have to go. Right now.'

'Chris?'

She shakes her head. Chris. No, not Chris. Danny breathes a

1

sigh of relief. At least this doesn't involve *him*. Let The Animal rot, please let him rot.

Mum points to his sports bag on the floor next to the bed. He is sitting up now, his mind racing. Hope has been lying curled up inside him so long, he hardly dares let it come to the surface. But you can't help it. To hope is to live. He looks inside. She's packed for him. Two, maybe three changes of clothes. His best. A few favourite belongings. What is this? Then he notices Mum's bag by the door. We're going somewhere, all right, but where? Hope and fear mix in equal measure. Why at this time? And why all the secrecy?

'Get dressed.'

Danny wriggles into his trackie bottoms and a shirt, before pulling on his socks and trainers. He takes his jacket down from the peg. Outside it's getting light. It's dawn.

'Ready.'

'Wait here.'

They are still talking in strained whispers. Leaving Danny watching from his bedroom, Mum steals across the tiny, cluttered living-room, darting a glance at her own room, and pulls a key from her pocket. She's going to the drawer. Chris's drawer. The one neither of them is allowed near.

No Mum, don't.

He knows what it means to touch something of Chris's. Terror. The ringing impact of a balled fist, the thud of a boot in the ribs. He or Mum, maybe both of them, cowering under the blows, waiting for it to end, the hard rain of fear.

The key turns.

Don't do it, Mum. You don't touch anything that belongs to Chris. Not ever. You can't!

But she does. All this time he's been willing her to be brave, to do something about Chris. But now it has come to the point, he is scared stiff, paralysed as much by hope as by fear.

Glancing a second time at her room where Chris is sleeping, Mum opens the drawer and takes something out. A bundle of banknotes which she stuffs into her jeans pocket. Danny marvels at the sheer cheek of it. She's tweaking the tiger's tail. He's heard something about that once. What was it about tigers? You can't skin them claw by claw. But that's just what

Mum is doing, she's skinning the sleeping Chris. She reaches in again and takes a second bundle, this time pushing it into her jacket pocket. She turns to look at Danny, flushed by her own act of courage, but as she does there is a noise from the room she shares with Chris.

'Cath? Cathy?'

Mum jumps, rapping her hand on the corner on the drawer. She winces. It's the hand Chris broke that time. It's never been quite right since. Danny sees the fear in her eyes, the way her body slackens with fright. He is used to this. Life these last few years has been like swimming in the dark, trying to fathom the murky depths, gingerly negotiating hidden obstacles, learning to survive in the currents and undertows that spell danger. He looks at Mum for a lead. She hesitates, trying to think. Then, waving him back from the door, she hurriedly pulls off her shoes and strips to her underwear. Out of respect, Danny turns away quickly. Mum grabs the dressing-gown that's lying over an armchair and slips it over her shoulders, hastily knotting the belt.

'I'm here.'

'What are you doing, Cath? Come back to bed.'

Mum exchanges an agonised look with Danny, then goes in to Chris. Her voice is soothing, reassuring. It is also false. Danny knows it, even if Chris is too stupid to work it out. Everything is fine, she's telling him in that gentle tone, nothing to worry about. Danny picks up snatches of conversation.

Chris's gruff burr: 'What were you doing?'

Mum's soft reply: 'Couldn't sleep . . . something to drink . . .'

Mum has left the bedroom door ajar. Danny is able to hear the voices, but he can't quite make out what is being said. He hovers by the door, wondering what to do. We're going, he thinks, that's for certain. Excitement pulses through him. It's out there, freedom, the promised land. Mum's finally made her choice. Freedom. *The promised land*. But what now? What do I do with the bags?

Come on, Mum. Do I keep my clothes on? What if Chris gets up and sees me? He'll realise right away that I should be in my

3

school uniform. Won't he be suspicious? Come back, for goodness' sake. Tell me something.

But Mum doesn't come back. Danny is still swimming in the dark. The flat is quiet. Not a sound comes from the other bedroom. Danny goes to the window and pulls back the curtain. The early morning light is grey over the damp London streets.

Where are we going?

Are we going?

His watch alarm goes off, sending an electric shock of fright down his spine. He switches it off and holds his breath. Seven o'clock. The time he gets up for school. Usually. But there's nothing usual about this gloomy morning. He has been shaken out of his sleep by a woman with terrified, haunted eyes. He is a nightswimmer, edging his way forward. Into what: danger or salvation? Freedom seems so very far away. But at least it's in sight.

The bad times are over, the times when Mum had almost made herself an enemy by staying with him, The Animal.

We're going. At least, we're supposed to be. With enough clothes for a few days. But *are* we going? In his dreams the promise of freedom has been dangled so many times before, only to be torn away at the last minute. Is this the time we actually get past the front door? Don't back down, not now, not when we're so close. Mum, where are you?

The minutes go by. From time to time Danny consults his watch, uncertain what to do. The minutes crawl, and the bags are still there, in the middle of his bedroom floor.

Maybe I should push them under the bed. Just in case.

Or get out my uniform. Just in case.

In case of him: Chris, and his pale, suspicious eyes.

Then a thought: Abdul will be here in twenty minutes. Do I ring him on his mobile? Warn him off?

Danny stares out at the street, watching the early-morning activity, the first workers heading for the Tube. What now? Not a word from Mum. Just the uncertainty of a teenage boy pulled out of bed and left standing alone in his room, wondering what to do. Then he hears something. He steals to the door.

4

Mum.

She's fully dressed again. Her face is pale and anxious. The strain shows in the lines around her mouth, the way her eyes are reduced to brilliant points of fear. Danny goes to speak, but she presses a finger to his lips. Too risky. She picks up her bag. He takes his own in his right hand and follows. He hears Chris. For once the self-satisfied snoring of *that pig* is a reassuring sound. He isn't awake, not suspicious. Mum smiles and gives Danny's arm a squeeze before gingerly opening the door. They are about to step out on to the landing when the door buzzer goes. Danny speaks for the first time since Mum came out of her room.

'It's Abbie!'

Why didn't I ring him? He'd thought about it. If only he could turn the clock back. If only . . . Suddenly the world is sliding back into danger.

'Go!' says Mum. 'We've got to go . . . now!'

It's like the floor is tilting, the walls closing in. Everything distorts. The world in which escape is possible is disintegrating and another world is rushing up to meet it. This is Chris's world, the terror zone. But there is no way back. They're running down the first flight of stairs. As they turn to descend to the ground floor they hear Chris's voice from the flat.

'Cath? *Cathy!*'

From the sound of it he's already out of bed, looking for them. The penny's dropping. It has to be by now. Abdul is waiting by the front door.

'Danny, why aren't you in your uniform?'

It's Mum who speaks first. She almost pants out the words. 'No questions now Abbie, please.' She's holding him by both arms, her fingers digging into his flesh, as if spelling out the urgency of the moment. 'Danny won't be in today.'

Abbie goes as if to ask a question, but the words never come out. At that moment, they hear Chris's voice. It comes out half-roar, half-shriek of pain.

'*Cathy!*'

'Look, we've got to go.'

And they're running, leaving Abbie puzzled and confused behind them. They have just gained the corner when they hear Abbie's warning shout behind them. Mum glances round. 'Oh my God, it's Chris. He's coming.'

Danny follows her look. The world lurches under his feet. It's Chris all right. He's pulled on a pair of jeans and he's sprinting after them. He's shirtless and barefoot. But it's not his state of dress that concerns Danny. It's the look in his eyes, the same pale, blue eyes that have bored right through him every time he has been interrogated over Mum's whereabouts. He's like a wild animal, a predator who's been tormented, wounded. An angry, dangerous wild animal. 'Come back here. You hear me, Cath, you come back here right now.'

But mother and son are not going back. Though none of the people making their way to work around them know it, they're running for their lives. In their desperation to put some distance between themselves and Chris, they are swinging their arms, their few belongings smashing into people as they pass, causing a stir. They ignore the shouted protests.

'Run Danny, don't turn round,' Mum pleads. 'I won't go back. I refuse to be afraid any more.'

They're on the High Street heading for the tube. The pavement is crowded by now. At one point Danny stumbles into an elderly Asian man. Mumbling 'sorry' he weaves in and out of the crowd after Mum. And all the while he can hear Chris shouting after them:

'Cath, Danny, come back. We can work it out.' Then again: 'Don't do this.'

But they are going to do this. Freedom is up ahead of them, at the end of a train line. Danny doesn't want to work anything out, and nor does Mum.

If she can refuse to be afraid, then so can I. There's nothing to work out with the lean, blond man who has been manipulating their lives like a puppeteer. They've had enough of it, enough of Chris's fits of temper, enough of the fists and the boots, enough of the terror. But it isn't over. Chris is closing on them.

He has nothing to carry, nothing to hold him back. Unlike him, they've got their lives in their hands. Suddenly Danny hears a scream. Chris has made a grab for Mum and seized a handful of her jacket. She spins round, slamming into the newspaper stand outside the tube. Pain stabs through her damaged hand. The door is closing on the promised land.

Danny reacts instantly, swinging his sports bag. All his strength goes into this one instinctive act of refusal. 'I won't go back. You can't make me.'

It smashes into Chris's face, sending him reeling. Danny experiences the thrill of his power. All those times he has cowered, feeling his weakness, and now he's paying Chris back. Take that, Animal! Somebody screams, another starts shouting.

'Go Danny,' says Mum, wrenching herself free. 'Run!'

They're inside the tube station, heading for the barrier. That's where freedom begins, just beyond that steel rail. Suddenly Danny feels a rush of horror. His pass. It's in the flat. He wheels round, despair turning his legs to jelly. Chris has got to his feet and he is coming again, blood trickling from a split lip. The pale, blue eyes flash hatred. Alarm bells ring in Danny's head. There's no way they'll make it. There isn't time to put money in the machine and get a ticket.

'Mum, my pass,' he gasps.

'I've got it,' she yells, holding up her own pass and his. Danny looks at her with a new found faith. All the times he felt disappointed in her for staying with Chris; all the times he despised her weakness when she made excuses for him; there's no disappointment this time. She's planned this down to the last detail. 'Just keep going,' she cries.

And that's it. They're through. Behind them the two ticket inspectors are struggling with Chris.

'You need a valid ticket, sir.'

The words are so out of place, Danny laughs out loud. They're fighting with a half-naked madman and they want a valid ticket! Members of the public crowd round. He's crazy, a drug addict. Somebody call the police.

Mum and Danny exchange glances. They know he's neither. They know exactly what he is. But they're not joining in the heated discussion. They've got one purpose and only one. To run away. To be done with the nightmare that is Chris Kane. To catch the train and get away. Away from the fists, the boots, the terror.

Chris

It takes a single sentence to clear his head.

'Call the police somebody.'

Now he's thinking, not just driven by instinct. He masters the blind anger and gathers his thoughts. 'No need for that,' he says. 'Lovers' tiff, that's all.' He looks around the small crowd, smiling at them, trying to work the old Kane charm. 'You know how it is.'

It doesn't wash. They've just seen a half-dressed man slamming a woman into a wall, terrorising her. They've seen his rage. He holds his hands up, backing away from the ticket barrier. Getting arrested would do his case no good at all. Time to fight another day, Chrissie boy. The bird has flown the nest and there's no catching her now, not like this. No, she's well gone. If you want her back, you'll have to rely on your wits. But you *will* have her back. No doubt about that.

'Everything's cool,' he says. 'No need to involve the police.'

He scans the hostile faces. If only you knew, he thinks, if you just understood the dance she's led me. Everybody always takes the woman's side, even the coppers. A man doesn't even get a hearing. But there's no point trying to convince them. Their minds are made up. Time to back off. Keep your gun-powder dry.

'I'm going,' he said, making an attempt at humour. 'Look, this is me going.'

One of the inspectors blocks him. 'Sir . . .'

But the look in Chris's eyes says it all. Either you get out of my way, sunshine, or you'll regret it. The inspector sees it and thinks better of his actions. There's an edge about the man, a fierceness you don't argue with.

Chris walks away, back towards the flat. He earns a few more inquiring glances on the way, but he doesn't feel self-conscious in the slightest. One thing about Chris Kane, he has never doubted for a moment that he is right. One hundred per cent right. He is doing what a man has to do. What's the matter with these people? Haven't they seen a bloke without a shirt before? I didn't have time to make myself respectable, did I? I was fighting for what's mine. Chris sees the street door swinging open. You don't think you can get away from me that easy, do you Cathy? We're meant to be together. Nothing can keep us apart. No matter how far you run, no matter where you hide, I'll find you. As Chris goes inside the building he is aware of somebody watching him. It's that lad who calls round for Danny. The one he goes to school with. What's his name? Abbie, yes Abbie. Hope stirs. Maybe he can point me in the right direction.

'Any idea where they've gone?' he asks.

The boy backs away.

What have they been saying about me? All lies, you can bet on that. Blaming me for everything. That's what you get for putting food on the table and clothes on their backs. Keep your temper, Chrissie boy. No sense scaring him off. You might need him. But the boy is spooked. He isn't about to hang around. Pity. It would have been useful to have got to know him earlier. Then Abbie wouldn't be so suspicious.

'I only want to talk to them,' Chris says reassuringly. 'Sort things out.'

Abbie shakes his head and walks away. Chris's eyes narrow. Walk away from me, will you? Well, I'll be seeing you again, Abbie boy. Soon. Then we'll have a little chat.

Danny

The train is packed, so they stand, holding on to the straps.

'Where are we going?' Danny asks.

The promised land, tell me it's the promised land. They've talked about this: running. Mum's painted him pictures of a home without fear, a life without looking over your shoulder. He has hung on every word, hoped against hope that this time they would do it. This time they would be free. So many times he has wanted to scream at her, tell her she can't be a real mother, not if she stays with him, The Animal.

Mum glances at the other passengers. Danny knows what she's thinking. One of them might know Chris, tell him where they're going. It's crazy, of course. Out of all the people in London, what's the chance of any of these people with their set, anonymous faces knowing him? But that's how you become, when you live with somebody like Chris, when your life goes crazy. Danny remembers a snatch of an old song, one they churn out every Christmas, and it takes on a new meaning.

He sees you when you're sleeping. He sees you when you wake.

The thought makes him shudder.

'Mum, where?'

'Home. I mean . . .'

Danny frowns at this. For most of his life home has been the flat, for what it is. Two bedrooms, living-room, bathroom; situated above a video shop. What does she mean, *home*?

'It used to be home,' Mum says. 'We're going to my Mum's. Somewhere to hole up for a few days while we look for a place of our own.'

Gran's! Danny wonders for a moment if Mum's taken leave of her senses. Is *that* the promised land? Is that where freedom starts? He's been there, what, six, maybe seven times in his whole life. And not at all in the last three years. His grandparents are an accident of birth, they're not family. Not the way most people understand family. Since when has that dingy end-of-terrace been *home*?

'Why?'

'Danny, you know what Chris is like. We've got to get as far away as we can. Especially now we've got this.' She pats the pockets holding Chris's money. 'I wouldn't feel safe in London,' she says. 'He would always be out there, looking for us.'

Other people might think she was being paranoid. Why be frightened in London, a city of eight million people? Surely that's one place you can lose yourself. What would his chances of tracking her down there be? But Danny knows Chris. He knows the menace in his blue eyes, the power in his lean, hard

10

body. Most of all he knows the cold rage that burns inside him, the determination to keep what's his. And in Chris's mind, Danny and Mum are just that, belongings. Property of Chris Kane.

'But why like this, Mum? Why didn't you tell me in advance?'

'I couldn't take the risk,' she tells him. 'If you'd known, you might have given us away.'

'I wouldn't!'

'Not on purpose, Danny. I know that. But Chris has a way of picking things up. He's always been able to read you like a book.'

She's right, of course. He's let things slip more than once, little things that brought on a slap, or worse. Danny remembers the innocent mistakes that have led to Mum getting hurt. Like the time Chris stamped on her hand and broke it. Danny knows the guilt of being responsible for her pain. Chris has to be in control, and if you've got something planned that doesn't involve him, he flips. Just like that. Then the man who can charm the birds out of the trees becomes cold and hard. He becomes a monster.

'I just wish I could have told Abbie.'

'You'll be able to ring him,' says Mum. 'Just as soon as we get where we're going.' Her expression changes. 'Just don't tell him where we are.'

'Abbie wouldn't let on!'

'He wouldn't *want* to tell,' says Mum. 'Just like you wouldn't. But Chris has a way of getting things out of people.' Her mind is working overtime. 'Has Abbie got your number on his mobile phone?'

'Of course. It's in his directory.'

'Then he's got to remove it.'

'You mean I can't even talk to him!'

Mum smiles. 'Of course you can. But I don't want Chris getting your number. If he talks to you . . .'

Danny can feel his skin creeping. For a man like Chris, words are weapons. He can make you turn inside out, do anything to please him. He tortures you with words, slides them inside you like a scalpel, lets them burrow into your brain until you want to scream. And that's only part of the power of Chris Kane.

'I don't want him getting in touch. Abbie will have to memorise the number.'

Danny nods. He can hear it in her voice, that edge of fear. Even the thought of Chris having a mobile phone number is enough to make her hands shake.

'This is our stop,' says Mum, picking up her bag. She consults a train timetable. 'The next train goes in ten minutes.'

As they stand on the escalator which carries the tube passengers up to the mainline station, they look back, half-expecting to see Chris climbing after them. But there's no sign of him. They've won. They have, haven't they? Danny gives Mum a smile. She responds with a nervous giggle. 'What's the matter with the pair of us?' she says. 'After all, he isn't Superman.'

But there isn't much they wouldn't put past him. As they sit in the waiting area, Mum nursing her aching hand and Danny crushing an empty Coke can, they don't have much to say to each other. They spend their time darting glances at the crowds thronging the station. They're looking for a lean, blond man with piercing, light-blue eyes. They're looking for his face, his handsome, terrible face. They're looking for the face of terror. But he doesn't appear. They've done it. They've got away.

Mum speaks for both of them: 'We're free.'

Abbie

He's gone back inside. Abbie draws breath. Thank goodness for that. Danny's told him about Chris. For a moment he thought Chris was coming after him. But I'd have nothing to say to him. I don't even know where Danny's gone. Good luck to him wherever it is. Away from the danger. Away from The Animal.

Abbie pulls up the collar of his jacket and turns towards the tube. There's no point being late for school, even if your best mate has just done a runner. No, he may as well get in on time. Danny's bound to be in touch. Abbie fiddles with his mobile. And I've got his number. OK, so he's gone, but that doesn't mean we'll lose touch. We're mates. And friendship's for keeps. I'm there for you, Danny, no matter what.

Chris

The bitch!

Now that he's on his own he can vent his anger. He smashes his fist down on the desk. I'll catch up with you, Cath, be sure of that.

That's when he notices. There's a key sticking out of the drawer. That shouldn't be there. It was in my pocket. He feels a rush of fury.

She's been in my money drawer.

She's picked my pocket while I was asleep.

The bitch.

The thieving cow.

He wrenches open the drawer and cries out. There were five rolls of notes in here. Now there are only two. He's down at least a couple of grand. Where's my notebook? He runs his eyes down the scribbled accounts. That much!

She's taking the mickey, that's what she's doing. That'll teach you to put your trust in a woman, Chrissie boy. They let you down, every last one of them. She's done you up good style.

He goes into the bedroom and opens the wardrobe. She's taken a lot of her stuff, of course. But he destroys what's left anyway. It's as if, by ripping her belongings to pieces, he is smashing the distance between them, making her naked and vulnerable. He takes a pair of scissors to it, shredding each dress, each pair of jeans. He hacks at her raincoat, the one she wore the day they met. He pulls out the shoeboxes and breaks the heels off each pair. He shreds the tights still in their packets and piles them in the middle of the room on top of the rest. This is all that's left of her, the clothes she couldn't carry. He kicks the pile and groans. The illusion dies. He's no closer to her. He can kick her belongings but he's powerless to touch her.

And that is what he hates, the feeling of powerlessness.

But I won't be powerless for long. I'll find a way to track you down, Cath. You're mine, and Chris Kane always gets what's his. No matter where you are, no matter what it takes to find you, I'll be seeing you Cathy, maybe sooner than you think. Then we'll find out who's smiling. He crosses the living-room to the boy's room. There's more here. His clothes, books, games. He picks up a Gameboy and dashes it against the wall. You wait till I catch up with you, Danny boy. We'll play a game you'll never forget.

He rubs his cheek where the sports bag hit him.

Think you're big enough, do you Danny boy? Want to take on your uncle Chrissie? Think you're hard enough? Hardness doesn't come down to one lucky blow. It's about taking pain more than the other guy. And nobody can take pain like I can.

Chris stamps around the flat, cursing them, spewing out a stream of abuse, spitting out their names, promising revenge. They've made a fool of you, Chrissie boy, a woman and a fifteen-year-old boy. You fed them, clothed them, took them places, and look how they've rewarded you. They've thrown it right back in your face.

He goes to the window and looks down at the street. They'll be out there now, on a bus or a train, counting their ill-gotten gains. They think they're safe. They think they're going to make a new life. With my money! Well, think again. Nobody takes Chris Kane for a mug. Not you, Cathy, and not your snotty-nosed kid either. He's had his eye on the boy a while, watching him growing, filling out, beginning to pose a threat. So the little snake-in-the-grass has dared to raise his head.

Sooner than expected. Still, not to worry, Chrissie boy. It's just a little setback. Time to put on my thinking-cap. I'll come up with a plan, and when I do I'll come looking for you.

Then you'd better tread carefully.

Very carefully.

2

Danny

Now, after three hours, Danny is really beginning to feel it, the sense of freedom. All the way up Mum has been saying it: *I feel free*. But not Danny, not until now. He can't believe that it's all behind him. It was only yesterday that he was searching Chris's face for any sign of menace, the slow burn that would lead to one of his fits of temper. A child's tantrum, but a man's strength. Maybe it was all too much to hope for, the life he had with Mum before Chris came on the scene, a life without fear. It is only in the last half-hour of the train journey that he has started to smile and joke with Mum, and already they are approaching the station. He looks out of the window as they pull up along the platform.

'Do you remember it?' asks Mum. Danny looks down the platform at the mixture of Victorian brickwork and tacky 1980s refurbishment. There is something familiar about it, but not much. Either way, it doesn't look much like the promised land. 'Well, do you remember it?'

'A bit.'

But all that Danny really has in his mind is a sense of difference, of otherness. The housebricks here are red rather than grey, the style of the roofs is different too. It's nearly four years since they were here last. Danny remembers because he had just started High School. Four years ago! That was before Chris. The Animal came on the scene twelve months later.

15

Danny liked him at first, better than the other boyfriends, the losers who were put off by a woman with a growing son, men who came and went quicker than an order at McDonald's. Chris was fun then. He took them places, brought them surprise presents. It was a novelty, having somebody else around the flat, especially when he had a sense of mischief and a talent for playing practical jokes.

Danny actually watched Chris, thinking he might learn from him what it was to be a man. There was an energy about the place those first few weeks, a liveliness, lots of laughter. But that was before Danny got to know Chris. Really know him. A new man is on his best behaviour when he first comes on the scene, but once he has settled in you discover the real person behind the early smiles. When he moved in Chris was generous to a fault, but he was always going to want something in return. And once he got his feet under the table it began. Payback time. Then he wanted to know every detail of Mum's day. Danny's too. Suspicion would flare over the slightest inconsistency, any moment that was unaccounted for. Chris started to *own* you. That's part of the reason Danny hasn't been to see his grandparents for years. Once he'd moved in, Chris became your family, your *whole* family. He was jealous of any competition. Mum couldn't see her friends. She couldn't see her parents either. Chris never showed any interest in her past. In fact, from the very first, he refused to admit she had one. He was her past, her present, her future. The moment she mentioned her mum and dad he cut her off in mid-sentence. As far as Chris was concerned, Cathy's life started the day they met. Chris's possessiveness isn't the only reason Danny hasn't been to see them, of course. There's the other thing, the thing he has never quite understood, a definite coolness towards him. No, not from Gran. She doted on him. The frostiness was always on Grandad's part. In some ways, Danny's grandfather reminds him of Chris. He wants you to be like him, think the way he does. He wants to own you too. But he can't own Danny. Because he isn't one of them, he's different.

'Let's go,' says Mum. She sounds cheerful, almost skittish. As they make their way out of the station Danny bumps into her and she starts swatting him playfully, like a kitten with a ball of wool. Danny likes the way she's suddenly younger, more carefree. The years seem to be dropping off her, that look round the eyes, so haunted and cautious, has been replaced by laughter lines. She's allowing herself to believe. Maybe there will be a new beginning. Maybe freedom really does start here. Danny shoulders his sports bag. There is a downside though. He's got his new life, but what sort of life will it be without his friends, without Abbie, Mick, Ramila? Danny's starting to feel cut off. For all the relief of getting away from Chris, he is a fish out of water, gasping for air.

Mum's read his mind. 'Nervous?'

He's a fish out of water, gills opening uselessly, tail flapping feebly. Nervous doesn't even come close to describing how he feels. The joy of release starts to fall away as he thinks about the new life that is unfolding right here, right now. On the way up he has listened to the strange accents around him. This is it, he's been saying to himself, this is what I'll be hearing from now on.

'Let's get a taxi.'

Chris always kept tabs on their spending. He gave them pocket money, even Mum. Enough for the bills, and not much else. A taxi seems extravagant. We'd have paid for that, Danny thinks, paid for it with slaps and kicks and thumps. But maybe we won't have to. Not now, now that we're free.

'We can do what we want,' says Mum, patting the pocket where she's got Chris's rolled banknotes. 'We're in the money.' She sings a little song from an old musical: 'Money, money, money. Money, money, money.'

Danny smiles, but it's a strained smile. This scares him, the thought that they've taken Chris's dosh. There was the time they hired a video without asking him. Chris stamped on the remote control until it was smashed to pieces. Mum deserves the money, of course. She's worked for it as hard as Chris has, harder, because she's got hers honestly. But she's never been given enough to live on out of it. She's had to go begging for every penny she's spent. No matter who earned it, it was still Chris's. Everything was his. And if you didn't agree, there was a kick or a punch to remind you that he owned everything. Your body, your soul, all of you.

Danny and Cath get into the first taxi by the forecourt rank, a private hire cab with the phone number on the side.

'Where to, love?' asks the driver.

'Edgecliff estate. 1, Cork Terrace.'

'From the Edge, are you?' he asks.

'I was brought up there,' says Mum. 'Why?'

The driver glances at Danny, registers the one fact about the boy that is important above all others. At least to some. 'Oh nothing,' he says.

They climb a long hill leading from the station. Danny looks back. He imagines Chris climbing the hill, running up it, cheeks puffing. He imagines his eyes on fire with indignation and anger at the way they've treated him. But there's no way of tracking them down. Mum didn't go near her parents the whole time she was with Chris, and if she tried to so much as mention them Chris shut her up. He didn't meet them or even speak to them on the phone, not once in three years. So why worry? They've left their old life behind. Time to look forward.

'Cork Terrace, wasn't it?' the driver asks.

'That's right. Number one. Do you know it?'

'I know the area.'

And that's all he says. But it's the way he says it that makes Danny think. What is it about the Edge that makes it *known*? He tries to think back and something comes to him: an impression. When he was here last he got this feeling that he was being looked at. By the neighbours, by Grandad, by just about everyone. Like he was from another planet.

'Here we are.'

The cab has pulled up outside an end-of-terrace. Above the rows of houses that make up the Edgecliff estate is the long escarpment that gives the area its name. Danny looks up at the long, lowering hillside, the Edge Cliff as it is known locally. He's been up there with Mum on earlier visits. It's like being on top of the world. It's so high and windy it makes you dizzy. And a bit scared. On top of the world? Maybe at the end of the world would be better. Just for a moment Danny finds himself thinking: *out of the frying pan into the fire.*

HARRY

At the sound of the car engine, the small, wizened man looks up from his gardening. Who's this pulling up? Must be something to do with the Parkers. I hope it isn't their eldest. Nasty piece of work he is. Into drugs, I shouldn't wonder. Nobody else ever shows up in a taxi. Not round here. Harry's about to get back to his roses when something makes him take a second look. That boy in the back: it can't be. He puts his pruning shears on the garden wall and straightens up. He is looking with interest now. No, not interest. *Anxiety*.

She's never come back.

I thought we'd seen the last of her.

He remembers what she said the last time. That she wouldn't be back, not after what he said, not after the disgusting things he said about her and her son. She even told him he wasn't her dad any more. He was just a lousy bigot, not fit to have a family. Well, good riddance, he said. Who needs a daughter that brings the kind of grief she has? You've made your bed, girl, now you can lie in it. Joan didn't speak to him for days after the bust-up. She accused him of driving his own daughter away, their grandson too.

She actually said he wasn't a real man, and that no man worth the name would drive their own blood away. But it wasn't his fault, not in a month of Sundays. It was Catherine, her and that half-caste son of hers. He couldn't bring himself to say grandson. Joan did. She was too forgiving, too accepting. You've got to know right from wrong and what Catherine did, the way she brought that lad into the world, it was wrong. The boy's no grandson of mine, he thinks. A mistake. A half-breed. Product of a squalid, disgusting affair while she was still at school.

His insides turn at the thought of it, his little Catherine messing with some chancer when she should have been studying for her exams. She met him at that club at the other end of town, that West Indian fellow, where all the other slappers hang out. Just teen rebellion, Joan had said. He'd known what it was all along, pure wickedness. He's seen them, plastered in make-up, skirts up to their waists. Harry scowls. She can't have come back, not after all this time, not after what we said to each other. All those terrible things. We burned our boats. Surely she hasn't come crawling back.

'Hello Dad.'

He takes off his cap and wipes his forehead. Dear God, she has too. She's come crawling back with her tail between her legs, all right. He might have guessed. She was never going to stand on her own two feet, that one. She never could stick anything out, our Catherine, not school, not the scandal of getting pregnant at sixteen. Not London either, by the look of it. So here she is, with her begging bowl at the ready, wanting a hand-out.

'Hello Catherine.'

'I've come to visit,' she says.

Her voice sounds shaky, as if she's unsure of her welcome. Well, you should be, young lady. You call me all sorts and then back you come, wanting to sponge off me again. He wants to tell her to get back in that taxi and go. But he can't do it. His life won't be worth living if he does. However much he wants to send her and that mistake of a boy away, he can't. Joan would make his life a living hell.

'You'd best talk to your mother then,' he says. 'She's inside.'

And that's it. Pulling his cap down, he goes back to his pruning. Not once in the brief conversation has he looked at Danny.

Danny

Now I remember, thinks Danny. So that's it. That's why they were all looking at me years ago. He sees himself reflected in the front window. Where they live – where they *used* to live – in a down-at-heel district of north London, almost every other face is one of colour, whether people were black, Asian, Turkish, Arab. Ethnic minorities, one of their teachers once called them. But they aren't a minority at all. Since when was half a minority? And since when did being born in Britain make you ethnic? Such a stupid word, eth-nic. What's it supposed to mean, anyway?

Danny hasn't thought about it much: race, colour. It only really mattered when somebody threw it in your face. Then it became something to defend, to stand up for. He's heard about it on TV and read about it in the paper, of course. There have been people who've told him it is his identity, his culture even. Occasionally there was a lesson on it at school, but it didn't seem that important really. What's the big deal about where people's families came from? They're here and that's that. It's too much a fact of life to get excited about. But it must be different on the Edge. He was too young to really understand it the last time, but it's obvious now. He hasn't seen a single black face since they got off the train. Is that what the taxi driver meant when he asked if they were from the Edge? Yes, he was too young to know why Grandad looked at him like that, why he sat in his chair staring at the television, why he hardly had a word to say to Mum or to Danny. He still doesn't understand, not in his heart. But even then Danny knew he wasn't wanted. Not really. Not by the bitter old man who could barely bring himself to speak directly to his own grandson.

'Some welcome,' says Danny, angry at the stupidity of it all. Promised land!

'Ignore him,' says Mum. 'At least he didn't cause a scene.'

Danny gives a brief nod. What's done is done. They had to get away from Chris. But to this? He looks up at the Edge Cliff and frowns. He has always associated this bleak hillside with his Grandad's cold, hostile stares. On the way home he would wonder what was the matter. Was his nose running? Was his fly open? Had he said something to upset the old man? Now he understands why people stared and why his Grandad hung back, a tic in his temple. I'm at the end of the world all right, thinks Danny, where the colour of your skin still makes a difference. Mum gives Gran a call.

'Mum, are you there?'

There is a crash. 'Cathy? Is that you, love? Oh, please say it is you.'

'Of course it's me. I've brought Danny up to stay.'

Gran comes hurrying from the kitchen, wiping her hands on her skirt. Her welcome couldn't be more different from Grandad's. 'Let me look at you. Oh Danny, the size of you! You've turned into a fine, young man. Oh Cathy, I can't believe it's been so long – four years!' She could have added *four wasted years*. She hugs Danny and plants a kiss on each cheek. Danny's face burns. Tears spill down her face. 'You don't know how many times I've looked up that street, willing you to come home. I've been so worried. The things that go through your mind. Cathy, why didn't you write, why didn't you phone?'

Danny wants Mum to explain, to tell her about Chris, but that can wait. After the way Grandad has greeted them it's a relief to be wanted, to be loved.

'I'm sorry,' says Mum.

'No, no,' Gran replies. 'You're not the one who should be sorry. Your dad . . . the stupid, stupid man. But you've just got to ignore Harry. That's what he's like. He can't change.' She shakes her head. 'It's the way he was brought up. His mother and father were the same.'

Excuses, thinks Danny. Just excuses. He doesn't see me. He sees my skin.

'Narrow-minded,' says Gran. 'Like this place.' She points at the rows of terraced houses clinging to the hillside. 'I've lived here over thirty years and I've never felt at home. Narrow minds, narrow lives.'

Danny sees something in her eyes. There's a yearning, a sense of hope snuffed out. Mum said something once, about how Gran made one mistake and got trapped into a dead-end marriage. Then Gran realises that she's talking too much.

'Come in,' she says. 'You must be tired. Put your bags down.' She inspects their luggage. 'You haven't brought much with you. How long are you staying? Don't tell me you've got to rush back. Not after all this time.' She hesitates, producing a handkerchief from her sleeve and gives her nose a long, hard blow. 'How long can you stay, Cathy?'

'I don't know, Mum. As long as you'll have us.'

A change comes over Gran. She realises this is more than a family visit. For the first time she looks into her daughter's face and sees the hurt written there. It's as if it's tattooed on her skin: the beatings, the broken hand, the terror. Gran's voice changes:

'What's happened?'

'It doesn't matter. I'll tell you soon, but not now. Danny and I, we're going to make a new start.' Gran looks at their scant belongings. 'We're not asking for charity.' Mum peels off a few ten pound notes from the roll in her pocket. 'We can pay our way.'

'You can put that away,' says Gran. 'I'm not bothered about money. I'm just glad to see you. You're sure there's nothing I should know? There's nothing wrong?'

Danny looks expectantly at Mum. How's she going to field this one? 'No, there's nothing wrong. Like I said, it's a new start.'

The two women look at each other for a few moments. The silence makes Danny uncomfortable. The only sound is of Grandad stamping the soil off his boots as he finishes his gardening. Instead of joining them he walks into the front parlour and opens the newspaper noisily.

'Silly old fool,' says Gran.

Mum and Danny exchange glances. Nobody is disagreeing.

Cathy

She goes to the back door and steps outside. In the small backyard, smaller than she remembers, she feels the whipping breeze against her face. She looks out at the patch of spare ground where she used to play as a little girl, pounding a tennis ball against the outhouse wall. She looks up at the Edge Cliff. That's where she ran, the day she found out she was pregnant, so afraid, so alone. Up to the hillside overlooking the town, and that's where she broke her heart. And I've been breaking my heart ever since, thinks Cathy, clinging to any man who'll have me, then wondering why it always goes wrong. But it has meant breaking Danny's heart too. Poor Danny, and all because I had to get away from this place.

Cathy glances indoors. Mum is making a cup of tea, Dad is sulking behind his paper. She knows what they'll be thinking. Especially him. Our Catherine has messed up again. Well, maybe I have, she thinks. But isn't this what you're for, Dad? You and Mum, you're meant to be a refuge, somewhere safe when things go wrong. Cathy realises she hasn't been quite straight with Danny. They *didn't* have to come here. They didn't need a bolt-hole. They've got Chris's money. No, it's more than that. In spite of Danny's unconditional love, she has been lonely for so long. The man she thought she loved took everything from her, even her self-respect. Cathy wants to be somewhere she can call home, just for a while. Mum can give her that, but can Dad?

She sees Danny standing in the kitchen and she aches inside. Sometimes, when I was looking out for my own happiness, I almost forgot you existed.

Danny looks much younger than his fifteen years, a little boy lost. She wonders if she's done the right thing by him, coming back here. It didn't matter in the part of London where they lived, her son's history. That she was a single mother, pregnant while still at school, that his father was black. It wouldn't matter in any one of a score of other places. Normal places, open-minded places. The country's moved on. But not all the country, maybe not even the majority of it, and certainly not the Edge.

She knows her home town very well. It's a throw-back. Prehistoric Britain. Narrow-minded, Mum said. Well, she hit the mark there. Cath remembers how desperate she was to get away, to escape from the whispers, the knowing looks, the twitching net curtains. Most of all from Dad with his ugly insults. She did get away, carrying her newborn son in her arms. Now she's back with that son, almost an adult; a couple of changes of clothes, a wad of banknotes and not much else. Back to face the music. A wave of panic sweeps over her. She will have to relive it all, what Dad calls the disgrace. I can't do this! In London, there was no disgrace, nothing to be ashamed of, just a mother and her child trying to make their way in the world. No, I really can't do this.

But she will have to. She will have to swallow her pride. She will have to put up with her Dad's innuendoes, the neighbours' knowing looks. Well, let them think what they want to. If this is what it takes then this is what's going to be done.

HARRY

I might have known, he thinks. Joan's at it already, killing the fatted calf. She'll have the best crockery out for tea, you watch. You wouldn't think Catherine had brought disgrace on this house. He remembers going into work as her condition started to show. Your girl got a bun in the oven, some of the younger men asked. He scowls. No respect, that's the trouble.

They don't care how they speak to you. No respect, no decency. He flicks his newspaper angrily, making it snap. He'd always felt so superior, commenting on them, all the stupid little people who failed. Then Catherine had to drag the family down to their level. What did he ever do to deserve this? He paid his stamp, worked every day of his life, never asked for anything from anyone. But did it do him any good? Did it heck as like! His only daughter in the family way by some . . . he wants to say the words out loud, shout them in the silly little cow's face, but you can't even do that these days. Country's overrun. An Englishman can't even voice his own opinions without being shouted down. Political correctness gone mad. Everything . . . everything gone mad.

He looks at the clock. Half-past five. They will be eating at six. He puts his paper down wearily. He knows that Joan will seat him next to Danny, her idea of getting him to build bridges. Well, do what you like, you're not getting me to play ball. You've got to know right from wrong, and bringing a kid into the world with no husband and no way of providing for it, what kind of behaviour is that?

He walks over to the window and looks out. He sees the street where he's lived for the last thirty-one years. He remembers bringing his wife here, then a few months later pushing his new baby girl in the pram, as pleased as punch. He remembers all the women leaning over the pram, cooing at his little princess. Life seemed so complete. The hopes he had for her, the dreams. She'd go to college, become a teacher, a doctor, do all the things he'd never done. And now look at her! No home, no job and a son who . . . he remembers what his dad always said: a white man can walk down a white street and a black man can walk down a black street. But where does a boy like Danny walk? It's not right, not natural.

He hears his name being called: 'Ready for your tea, Harry?'

He shakes his head slowly. Ready? I'll never be ready, not for something like this.

Chris

Two hundred miles away, Chris is sitting among the shredded clothes, the broken shoes, the old documents and photographs. A frenzy has seized him. He's got to find something, anything, to track her down, to get back what's his. He's been robbed. They've both gone, his woman, his money. It hurts too. How's a man to be measured? By the woman on his arm and the cash in his pocket. It's what gives Chris Kane his pride. He can always pay his way. He never needs to ask for anything from anybody. But now he feels numb, gutted. The flat is empty without her. He pictures her face and feels sorry for himself. He's never loved anybody like Cathy. She's needed correcting from time to time, of course. What woman doesn't? But everything he has done, he's done for her own good. Why couldn't she understand that? Why couldn't she appreciate everything he has done for her? He holds up a photograph, the one of them at his brother's wedding. What more proof does she need? We were made for each other, Cathy. So how could it all go wrong?

He gets up and goes over to the drawer. He still can't believe it, first that she could steal from him, second that she would *dare* to. Didn't he make it clear what happened to anybody who messed with his property? What does she think he is, a soft touch? Well, forget it Cathy. You're not going to get away with it. You won't get one over on Chris Kane.

He puts the photograph in his wallet then goes into the kitchen and comes back with a black bin bag. He starts stuffing the pile of torn and smashed belongings into it. Nothing there to give him a clue to her whereabouts. When he started going through her things he was convinced he'd find something, like one of those forensic scientists. Systematically, bit by bit, he would build up a picture of his loved one's movements. It hasn't happened.

'But I'll come up with something,' he says aloud. 'Be sure of that.'

He ties the bag and puts it by the door. He surveys the flat. There's got to be something here, anything that can tell him where she's gone. He'll do the rounds, of course, visit all her friends, not that she really had any left. He saw to that. But she's not stupid. She'll have covered her tracks well. She won't just sit there waiting for him. Crafty, that one, brains to go with the looks. That's what attracted him to her. She knows what's coming to her, all right. No, he'll have to get his thinking cap on if he's going to get her back.

Come on now, Chrissie, think.

Think.

Danny

His mind is racing.

So much has happened in just a few hours. He has felt so many emotions today. There was fear and bewilderment when

Mum woke him to tell him they were going. Then there was the exhilaration of their flight, the way they escaped Chris's clutches. He finds himself smiling at the mental picture of Chris taking one in the kisser. I did that, thinks Danny, I landed him one smack in the face. All the times he felt like a little boy, standing helplessly by while that thing, that Animal, hurt his mother. Suddenly he had stood up for her. But that seems a long time ago. The buzz that impossible act of courage gave him has faded. Too many other things have tainted it already – discovering why Grandad won't look at him, realising that the promised land is a foreign land and he is alone in it. Now the doubts are beginning to come. Danny sits up on the camp bed.

His room is empty except for a couple of suitcases, a broken sewing-machine, some bags of material. Rain is pattering against the window-pane. He has phoned Abbie. It was strange not to be able to tell him where he was. He told Abbie to memorise his number then take it off the directory. Chris Kane hung like a phantom between them. They spoke for a few moments, not really sure what to say to each other, then hung up. Now he is wondering where he will find another friend like Abbie. Sitting here in the darkness of this empty room he is scared of his freedom, apprehensive about this promised land on a hill.

He feels more alone than he has ever felt in his life. Somehow, even being safe and free doesn't quite make up for that.

3

Danny

Up on the Edge it's as though you can see the whole world. Danny runs to a point where the wind-scoured ridge falls away steeply towards the squat, uniform houses of the Edgecliff estate. For the first time since he arrived, he feels a sense of excitement. Back in London you never seemed to see further than the end of a traffic-clogged street. The highest he can remember being was in the grounds of Alexandra Palace. His mind goes back to a bright summer's day when they had a picnic there, just him and Mum. He says the words as if reciting a magic spell: *Ally Pally*. It was a day without clouds and they walked for hours just enjoying being alive. That was before Chris of course, before he started owning them, before they learned to live without being alive.

'What's that?' he asks, pointing out a monument in the distance.

Mum catches up with him. She was as keen as Danny to come on this walk, away from Grandad and those meaningful looks. Just being out of that house and here, in this ever-so-slightly disappointing promised land, she seems younger somehow. 'What are you looking at?'

'That monument, like an obelisk.'

'Oh, the war memorial. It's from the Second World War. Edgecliff boys who died on the battlefield. Strange how something so beautiful can come out of something so terrible.'

Danny wonders if one day they will think of their own lives like that: beauty out of terror. 'Are you sure he can't find us?' Danny asks. There's no need to ask who he means.

'I'm sure,' says Cathy. 'I spent weeks preparing this. It used to upset me that he didn't want to know where I was from. It's turned out to be a blessing in disguise.' She pauses. 'Danny, do you blame me for what's happened?'

Danny reacts almost angrily. As if he ever could. All his life she has been everything to him. Part of his anger is that somebody so beautiful and loving could get herself involved with somebody so . . . he can't think of the words. There is only one word for Chris – Animal. 'Never!' he says fiercely.

'Sure?'

'Of course I'm sure. You weren't to know what he was like.'

'It doesn't stop me feeling guilty.' Danny shrugs. It's his way of telling her to change the subject. 'Do you want to see the school?'

Danny's heart tugs. The thought of starting a new school has brought him up short. It tells him that their move is permanent, or at the very least long-term. Abbie and his friends recede into the shadows. He remembers his first day at High School: the uncertainty, the rush of panic, the sensation of being a little cork bobbing on an enormous tide and something tugs in his heart.

'There, just beyond the dual carriageway. It's that T-shaped building. That's where I went to school.'

And where you discovered you'd got pregnant with me, thinks Danny. She told him the story one rainy day in their flat, how she had to run out of German to throw up in the school toilets. After that everyone knew. You were another schoolgirl pregnancy.

'You'll be starting a week on Monday, after half-term. I've already arranged the transfer.'

Danny looks at her. 'You've been in touch with the school?'

'Yes, a couple of weeks ago.'

'You really did have everything planned, didn't you?'

Mum looks a little shamefaced, as if she has betrayed him. 'I couldn't tell you, Danny. You don't know how hard it was. But if you'd let it slip . . .'

Danny's forgiving. He's in the promised land, even if it isn't quite what he was expecting. 'It's all right, Mum. You were doing the thinking for the both of us. You did the right thing.' He speaks reassuringly: 'You always do.'

He says it without a trace of irony. OK, so he has been uprooted, taken away from his friends, and that's hard. But life with Chris had become worse than hard. It was intolerable, especially for Mum. The intervals between Chris's outbursts were becoming shorter, the happy times harder to remember. When Danny thinks about it, he remembers his life with Chris as a long corridor with doors on either side.

Living with The Animal was like walking down that corridor, praying that the doors wouldn't open, that you would get to the end without being challenged by him. Danny relives the feeling of tiptoeing, as if crossing a surface made entirely of eggshells, praying you wouldn't make a floorboard creak. You almost reach the end. Your heart is thumping, a heat rash is spreading over your back and neck. So close. Almost free. But as you dare to hope you're safe the very last door flies open and he's there, his pale blue eyes looking right through you. Then you know, the terror is about to begin.

'We're going to make it, you know,' Mum says, scattering his thoughts.

'Yes, of course we are.'

In a way, they've made it already. They've broken away. They've finally got to the end of the corridor and walked out into the light of day. Is it any wonder they still find themselves astonished and slightly blinded by the brilliance of freedom? So I've got to start a new school, thinks Danny. That's nothing compared to staying with Chris. With him out of the picture, the last obstacle has gone, the last obstacle to becoming a man.

Chris

He stands in the middle of the living-room, hands on hips. He has been over the flat with a fine toothcomb. Nothing. Not a phone number, not a photograph from her life before him, not a single pointer to where she's gone, her and the brat.

'Bitch!'

He imagines the surprise on her face when he tracks her down and he finds himself smiling at the thought of it. Then he remembers his fruitless search and the smile fades. What if he doesn't find them? What if she's gone for good, her and the money? Stop it, Chris, he tells himself. You'll track her down. There isn't a woman born who can put one over on Chrissie Kane. No, you'll come up with something. Mr Resourceful, that's what his mates call him. He looks around the flat. There's got to be something she's missed. You can't live in a place this long without leaving something of yourself behind. No matter how long she planned this, she's got to have overlooked something.

'But what?'

He walks from room to room opening drawers, picking up ornaments, running his fingers along surfaces. Still nothing.

He imagines her doing exactly this, walking round the flat while he was out, painstakingly and systematically removing anything that might lead him to her. And didn't she make a good job of it! She did it all without once arousing his suspicions.

'I never dreamed you had it in you, Cathy.'

For a few moments he almost admires her. Then he remembers the money, the betrayal of trust. He has never loved anyone the way he loves Cathy. He loves her so much he *is* her. That's why he can't let her go, because if he does he is allowing part of himself to die, the part that makes things happen, the part that takes control, the man part.

'I can't let it happen, Cathy,' he says. 'Nobody walks away from me. Nobody!'

He reinforces the sentiment by hurling a coffee mug against the wall. He'll have her back, even if it means taking her back in little pieces. He feels the fragments of coffee mug under his foot and smiles. Free and whole away from me, or broken with me?

'No contest,' he says with a second, humourless smile.

Then it comes to him. Of course, the school. They'll have transfer records. All he's got to do is call in and see the secretary. He laughs out loud. 'Why didn't I think of it before?'

He's been along to parent's evening. OK, so it was only the once when he was still trying to impress Cathy with his thoughtfulness. But for three years he's been Danny's Dad in all but name. He'll have no problem sweet-talking the details out of the headteacher or the secretary.

'Chrissie,' he chuckles, 'You genius you.' He flops down in his favourite chair and takes out the photo of him and Cathy that he keeps in his wallet. 'See you soon, lover,' he says. 'See you soon.'

Cathy

'We're back,' she calls as they walk through the door.

Mum appears from the kitchen, wiping her hands. Cathy smiles. That's the way she always imagines Mum. In the kitchen, washing something, making something, waiting on the old grouch hand and foot. She has always understood it, of course, Mum's need to *keep busy*. Because, if she ever stops, she will have to face the truth about her cheerless straitjacket of a marriage. So long as you're on the go you don't think, you don't cry. We're not so different, thinks Cathy. We both live through stupid dreams. With you, it's hearth and home. With me, it's the great romance.

'Had a good walk?' she asks.

'Yes, it's blown the cobwebs out. Some view, isn't it Danny?'

Danny nods. Typical teenager. Why say a word when a nod or a shrug will do? 'I showed him the High School.'

'Oh, you're putting his name down then?' asks Mum, pleased as punch.

'I already have,' says Cathy.

'It's not such a bad school,' says Mum. 'Our Cathy went there.' Her expression changes. Both Cathy and Danny know what she's thinking. *Until that business.*

Until Cathy fell pregnant.

'Still, got to get on.' She reaches the door then turns round. 'Michael Lomas is at the High,' she says.

'Michael?'

'Pat Lomas's boy. He'll be about thirteen. I sent you the bit in the *Chronicle*. You know, he won that prize. Bright boy, Michael.'

Cathy sees Danny looking. 'Pat Lomas was my best friend at school,' she explains. 'Mum used to send me any news . . .' Her voice trails off. A shadow has fallen over her. Oh my God, she thinks. I thought, after all the times I let Danny down I'd finally done something right. I thought I'd remembered everything. But I haven't.

Not everything.

Chris

He has been waiting all weekend for this moment.

Now, as he knots his tie and slips on his sports jacket, he smiles. You scrub up nicely, Chrissie Kane. You look quite the upstanding citizen. He adjusts the tie again, feeling slightly self-conscious. Stupid palaver, all this. But if he's going to tease the information he needs out of that school he's got to play the part. Doting father, loving husband, that sort of thing. He tries his expressions out in the mirror. Concern for the boy, anxiety over what they're living on, eagerness to have them back, he executes them all perfectly. Deserves a rotten Oscar! He knows exactly what they're living on, of course. His hard-earned dosh. Not to worry, Chrissie boy, you'll have them back soon enough: Cathy, the brat and what's left of the money. Anything they've spent he'll take out of their hides, just so they don't try it again.

It's one stop on the tube. He sits counting the minutes, savouring the expectation. Soon he will have the details in his hot, sticky hand. Then we'll see, Cathy. We'll see who's got the upper hand. The woman opposite is looking at him. He smiles and she smiles back. She's quite a looker, not a patch on Cathy, but pleasing enough to the eye. No sense trying to take it any further, though. Chris Kane is a one-woman man, and in a few minutes he will have his one woman in his sights. He imagines himself shooting clay pigeons. Pull. Aim. Gotcha! He walks up the street to the school. Maybe he should have phoned first and made an appointment. Still, what's a few minutes' wait? She's worth it, his Cathy. She's beautiful. He remembers one time when he loved her so much he thought he'd choke. He'd given her a slap. Nothing heavy, you understand, nothing that would leave a mark, just a reminder who was boss. She looked up at him through her tears. God, she was never so lovely as when her face was streaked with tears. He found that very vulnerable, very *feminine*. For crying out loud – he loves the girl! Love is taking over somebody so completely there is hardly anything left of them. But he can't have loved Cathy enough. He's left something of her intact, something that refuses to be taken over, something that has not been absorbed into his world. That something has lain hidden, like a time-bomb, waiting to blow up in his face. Once he has found her he will never make that mistake again. He won't let her out of his sight. That's always been my trouble, he thinks. To damned soft. Well, no more Mr Nice Guy.

He reaches the gates. What's this? Locked! He checks his watch. Ten o'clock in the morning. So what's it doing locked? He sees somebody up a ladder replacing a broken window. 'Excuse me, mate,' he says. 'How come the gates are locked?'

'Half-term,' says the glazier. 'Do you want me to give the caretaker a shout?'

Chris's disappointment is crushing. Half-term. Fancy forgetting that. Cathy had been talking about it just before she cleared off, asking if they could go to Laser Quest or down to the Arsenal so Danny could see his heroes. Another of her little tricks, lulling him into a false sense of security. He wants to scream. The deviousness of it! The two-faced dishonesty! Why didn't you talk to me, Cath? You only had to talk it through.

'No, no need to disturb him. Any idea when they reopen?'

'Next Monday, I think.'

Next Monday. The trail won't have gone too cold by then. No, Monday it'll have to be. Until then, Cathy, until then.

Cathy

She decides not to say anything to Danny. It isn't as if Chris is likely to find it. What reason would he have to pull back the carpet?

And yet . . . She can feel her neck burning at the thought of it. Chris didn't give her enough money as usual, so she had to buy a cheap carpet for the living-room and no underlay. That's why she lined it with newspaper. But why *that* newspaper, the one from Mum, the one with the article about Michael Lomas and his stupid prize? Couldn't she have foreseen this, that she might do a runner one day? She thinks of the name of the town, their promised land, their refuge, printed on the top right-hand corner of the page. Suddenly, it is as if she is a mobile camera moving upstairs, poking the lens into the flat. Now the focus is shifting to the floor. It is the same floor where she has lain rolled up, knees tucked into her chest, arms protecting her head. The floor where he has rained down kicks and punches. The floor where she has made terror's acquaintance. Now the lens is nudging its way under the corner of the carpet. She can hear the rustle of newspaper, like an insect.

She can see the edge of the yellowing copy of the *Chronicle*.

And there is Michael's photograph and the headline: *Edgecliff boy's achievement*.

Oh, but you're making too much of it. Why would Chris look under there? He isn't going to start rummaging under the carpets, now is he? He doesn't even know there's anything there. She is starting to feel better. No, the secret will probably lie hidden for years and by then she and Danny will have made a new life for themselves. She has half-persuaded herself that they're safe. That's right, Chris has never done a tap of housework or DIY. Why would he start now? The place is probably a pigsty already. No, no need to worry I'm sure.

She sees Danny watching TV and her heart aches for him.

I've got to be sure.

She remembers the way Danny hit Chris and she fears for her son. Because anything you do to Chris Kane he repays with interest. Cathy girl, you've got to be absolutely sure. There can be no comeback.

Sure, yes I'm certain there's no danger. Because if there was, if he came looking for us with revenge in his heart, God knows what he would do.

HARRY

The boy is in Harry's chair. Harry stops at the door, uncertain what to do. Does he make a fuss and have Joan on his back all night? Or does he just ignore it? But that will mean letting him take the house over. Harry glares at the boy's back, as if trying to shame him with his fixed stare. Typical of them, he thinks.

He's seen these coloured lads over on the north side of town, watched the way they act. They hang round in gangs, looking at you as though they own the place. It makes his blood boil. Their cheek, their insolence, their cockiness. He remembers what this town used to be like, before they started taking all sorts in. A charitable institution, that's all we are these days. Immigrants, asylum seekers, good old Britain will have them all and send them off to make their fortune with a juicy grant in their pocket. Anybody can come over here now with their begging bowl, expecting us to support them.

But this is my blood!

He moves into the living-room, eyeing the boy. The conflict has always been there inside him, that the boy was something wrong, but also in some way part of him. He tries of find something of himself in the taut, dark features. But what's there to recognise? All he can see is the father, that black fellow, the one who . . . He feels hot, suffocating with shame. How could she do it, how could his Catherine let herself down like that? How could she drag us all through the dirt?

The boy notices him. 'Hello Grandad.'

'Hello.'

He answers before he can think better of it. He's been giving the boy the silent treatment, but it's hard not to reply when somebody speaks directly to you. So he answers and sits down on the settee, still looking at his armchair.

'Sorry, have I taken your place?'

Harry hasn't been expecting this. The boy sounds almost respectful, not like the street gangs over on the north side.

'Well, it is where I usually sit.'

The boy gets up and they swop places. Harry feels the warmth of the boy's body still in the chair. My blood, he's my blood. But what does that mean? Harry hates all this, the confused feelings inside. This is your grandson, he thinks, your only grandson. But if the boy's very birth was wrong; if he crossed a line that was never meant to be crossed, then how can you really love him? How?

He sees Joan come into the room. She sees them watching television together and smiles. Don't get your hopes up woman, thinks Harry. I'm taking him in because he's Catherine's child and blood is thicker than water. But it's still bad blood.

Yes, that's it exactly.

Bad blood.

Danny

He looks around. It is one of the few times they have all been in the same room together. So this is it, he thinks, this is my family. My blood family, that is. He glances instinctively at the curtained window. Somewhere out there he has a father too. He can honestly say that it has hardly crossed his mind before. He's wondered about him, of course, what he looks like, where he works, if he has other kids, but he has never dwelt on it much, not the way they do in TV soaps. It has never got to be an obsession. Down in London it hardly seemed to matter. Him and Mum, that was all the family he needed. They were about as close as two people could get, two against the world. Even after Chris moved in, it got them through, the bond they had built up over the years. They looked out for each other. They shared an early-warning system that seemed to get them through most of Chris's moods.

'Would anyone like anything from the kitchen?' asks Gran. 'I'm making a pot of tea.'

'Not for me, thanks,' says Mum.

'What about you, Danny?' asks Gran.

He notices Grandad's head snap round. It reminds him of a squawky old parrot in a zoo. The thought makes him chuckle inside, but he knows better than to laugh out loud. Danny knows immediately what the old man's thinking. She's doing it again, putting the boy before him.

'A few biscuits,' says Gran, oblivious to Grandad's stare, 'a slice of carrot cake?'

'Go on,' says Danny, smiling, 'You've twisted my arm.'

'What about you, Harry?'

'Might as well, I suppose.'

For the grunted reply, read: *Oh, so you've remembered me then!*

What is your problem, thinks Danny? What's the big deal about me being black? Back home, every other person is. That's when he remembers the taxi driver, and his reaction when they asked for the Edgecliff. Maybe it isn't just Grandad.

Maybe there's a Britain I don't know, a Britain where it still matters about the colour of your skin. Back in London, he was vaguely aware of areas where there *was* a problem. Abbie talked about it. Ramila too. She mentioned Stephen Lawrence sometimes, and talked about whole districts where you didn't hang around, not if you knew what was good for you. Somehow, it never seemed real though. There were people who gave you dirty looks, old people usually, the odd copper. But they didn't chip away at his sense of belonging. Every Saturday Danny went down the market with Mum and they had samosa on toast from an Asian guy called John. That summed it up. Keep Britain White? England for the English? Stuff like that didn't mean anything, not when you could get samosa on toast. All that racism stuff was unreal, a complete joke. But it's real here, thinks Danny. I can feel it. It's built into the bricks of the place.

He finds himself looking at Grandad. What he sees is a man, old before his time, bitter for reasons Danny can't imagine, totally set in his ways. He has his own chair, his own place at the kitchen table, his own routines. Danny has learned that much already. But it is a man Danny sees, not a white man. So why can't he see *me* that way? A boy, just a boy.

Why should the colour matter? What is that? Biology surely, nothing else. What matters is, I'm your daughter's son. Doesn't that count for anything? Doesn't that push all the other stuff to one side?

Gran returns, handing Danny a plate with two slices of carrot cake and a couple of biscuits.

'You'll have his teeth rotten,' Grandad grumbles. For that read: *So why does he get his first?*

The intruder. The cuckoo in the nest.

Gran brings in the teapot and two cups on a tray.

'Where's my cake?' snaps Grandad.

'Oh dear, I quite forgot,' says Gran. 'I'll get you some.'

But, as she turns to go, Grandad shoves past her. 'Sit yourself down,' he says, 'I'll get my own.' Then, as he goes into the kitchen, a half-audible: 'I know where I stand.'

Gran exchanges a pitying look with Mum. They try to hide it from Danny, but he's picked it up. Some promised land!

4

Danny

It is Monday, his first full week of freedom, and Danny is running along the Edge. Chris isn't quite history; the memory of the kicks, the punches, the screams are just too raw for that. For so long Chris has cast a darkness of – there's no other word for it – evil over his life. You don't come out from under the shadow easily. But already scar tissue is forming. Loud noises don't make him jump quite the way they did. He feels no need to sneak into the new house, 1 Cork Terrace. The creak of the floorboards aren't magnified into gunshots by his fear of who is listening. He doesn't spend his time wincing in anticipation of another eruption of rage. He is even forgetting what it is like to tiptoe around another human being, wondering if your expression, your body language, just your being there will set him off. There is a peace inside Danny Mangam that he has rarely felt before, certainly not in the last three years, and nothing that Grandad can do will disturb it. Sure, Danny has to make concessions for the old guy. Around Grumbleguts he behaves in a way that is slightly guarded, but it isn't fear that makes him do it. It's concern for Mum. She wants a new life. She wants to leave her hell with Chris behind her. She wants the Edgecliff estate to be that promised land they dreamed about. So Danny does his best to ignore Grandad. It isn't that hard. The old guy's more clown than tyrant.

'Free-dom!'

41

Danny pounds along the Edge, feeling the north wind rush against his face and chest. He smiles. He loves the buzz he gets from running. He was the best distance runner in his old school. It was his respite from The Animal, his therapy. In the absence of any real countryside, they used to run along the canal towpath. It was quiet there, a little haven where the plant life was allowed to grow wild.

As you drove forward, concentrating on keeping an even stride, you could easily forget that you were in the middle of London. The traffic noise faded almost to nothing as you measured out the run from lock to lock. Danny's running had made him quite the celebrity, the 'Big Man' as Abbie put it. It made him popular with the girls too. His smile fades as he remembers. Of course, it was this weekend. He was going to ask Ramila out. In his excitement of the escape he has forgotten all about it.

'Ramila.'

The thought of her makes him run even harder, until he is sprinting. It's a stupid thing to do. By the time he reaches the war memorial he has almost made himself sick. There's a sour taste at the back of his throat. He spits, but it doesn't do the trick. He bends double, senses swimming, trying to get his breath back. But driving himself to the point of exhaustion and beyond has done the trick. When he finally straightens up, the sense of loss isn't quite so acute. He can almost think of Ramila without a ball of disappointment and longing forming in his guts. He sits down and pulls his mobile out of his jacket pocket.

'Abbie?'

'Hey Danny, how're you doing?'

'Not bad. I've got a few things in my room now. It looks a bit more like home.' He's kidding himself. The few things are a bed, an alarm clock and a lamp. He's still more a guest than a fixture. Mum says she's going to spend some of Chris's – *their* – money doing it up. 'So what are you doing?'

'Hanging round. We're on half-term.'

'Yes, I know. Me too. I start at my new school on Monday.'

Abbie goes quiet for a moment or two. Talk of a new school makes the move sound permanent. 'So what's it like?'

'I'll tell you on Monday. I haven't even been inside the place yet.'

Danny looks at the T-shaped building in the distance. The thought of walking through the gates is unsettling. 'Seen Ramila?'

'Yes, last night. We were all hanging round the tube.'

'Has she been asking after me?'

'What do you think?'

Danny's heart leaps. 'What did she say?'

'She just wanted to know where you'd gone. I said it was a secret. I explained about The Animal.'

Danny digs his heel into the thin turf. Chris. He's the one to blame for all this, the acid that ate through the tissue of his life. 'Tell her I haven't forgotten her,' says Danny. 'You'll see me again. Soon.' Abbie doesn't say a word, but it's obvious what he's thinking. 'I'll call again,' says Danny, less convincing because he's repeating himself. Then that word: 'Soon.'

He starts jogging down the hillside towards home. No, he's going to need another word for his grandparents' house. How can that be home? He has just called home. He thinks of Chris. *Some* kind of home.

He wonders if he will ever have a real home.

Chris

Chris gets up late. There isn't much to get up for. Look at this place, he thinks, it's a tip. Cathy should be here, putting it straight. Does she really think a man ought to live like this? He swings his legs over the side of the bed and pushes back his hair. It feels lank and greasy. Time I got it cut, he thinks. Cathy would have reminded me, if she hadn't . . . he looks at her side of the bed, imagining her there, legs curled up almost to her chest. She always slept like that, in a rolled-up ball, just like a hedgehog. And didn't his little hedgehog have spikes! He thinks about his money.

43

She knew exactly how to hurt him. He pads across the floor in his bare feet. He knows he will have to go out soon, do some business, fill the hole she has made in his finances.

He showers and then crosses the living-room to make some breakfast. The dishes are still in the sink. He hasn't washed up for two days. He has to rinse a bowl and a spoon so he can have cereal. As he munches his Special K, a legacy of Cathy's flirting with a healthy lifestyle, he runs down the list of what he's lost. Two things come top, a woman who was beautiful enough to make other men jealous, and a wad of cash most of them would die for. On two counts she has robbed him blind.

'The bitch!'

He is going into the living-room when he catches his toe in the corner of the carpet. He stumbles and is barely able to keep his footing. He kicks the carpet back angrily. That's what comes of buying cheapo carpet. Couldn't she have come up with something better on the money he gave her? He finds himself wondering what she spent the housekeeping money on. He has always harboured suspicions about what she got up to when she was out of the flat. That's why he kept such a tight rein on her. He glances at his watch. I'll tack it down later, he thinks. First I've got to earn some readies. You're nothing without the folding stuff.

HARRY

The boy arrives back from his run flushed and sweaty. Harry watches him from the backyard where he has been fixing Joan's washing line. If he's told her once, he's told her a dozen times. Don't hang all the bedding on it at once. It just won't take the weight. The boy opens the fridge and starts drinking milk straight from the carton. Look at him. Just look at the young beggar, swigging it down like he's paid for it. No thought about people having to drink after him, either.

'Can't you use a glass?' grumbles Harry.

'Oh, I didn't see you there.'

Too right you didn't. But I'm keeping an eye on you. 'I don't care what they do down in London,' grumbles Harry, 'in this house, you drink from a cup or a glass.'

Harry detects a snort of annoyance. The boy pours the milk into a glass. He shakes the last drop out of the carton. It's empty. 'Sorry,' he says, dropping the carton in the bin. 'I was really thirsty. It's the running.'

Harry yanks on the washing line and secures it to a rusting iron hook that is jutting out of the brickwork. Irritation oozes from every pore. 'We all get thirsty,' he says. 'Just remember there's more than you in the place.'

'Sorry Grandad.'

That's right, thinks Harry, you're good enough at saying sorry, but meaning it is a different matter. That's the trouble with the world these days. Everybody says they're sorry, but nobody means it. If they were, they wouldn't do the things in the first place. The boy wouldn't swig straight out of the carton, Joan wouldn't snap the washing line, Catherine wouldn't have got herself pregnant.

Sorry? They don't know the meaning of the word.

Cathy

She arrives back flushed and happy. The first job she's applied for and she's been successful. OK, so it's only serving in a bakery-cum-café, but it's cash in the pocket, enough to pay Mum something for their keep. It means she can hang on to the cash she took from Chris, put it towards something they need. Most of all, it means standing on her own two feet, not beholden to anyone. Not to Mum, not Dad, most of all not a man who wants to own her. I'm not useless, she thinks. I'm not just the woman who's messed up her life, then messed up her son's to boot. I can do something, I can put it right.

'You look pleased with yourself,' says Mum.

'I am,' says Cathy brightly. 'I've got myself a job.' It sounds good. *I've* got myself a job. Just like, *I* got my son away from the psycho. *I'm* starting to make a life for the two of us. Mum looks delighted. Cathy has no problem reading her. It's more proof that they intend to stay, that maybe all those lonely times are in the past. She can have some sort of family again. Somebody besides bitter, brooding Harry. 'Where's Danny?'

'He's just got back from his run,' says Mum.

'Danny,' says Cathy.

'Yes?'

'I've got something for you.' She hands him a large carrier bag. It's a big deal to her, as if she is handing him a new life, trying to make up for the bad times.

'What is it?'

'Take a look.' He examines the contents of the bag. 'It's your new uniform.'

He looks less than thrilled. 'Yes, I figured that out.'

Cathy is willing him to like it, to look forward to his new school. She wants all that stuff she dreamed about to come true, a new start, freedom, the promised land. 'Why don't you try it on?'

'Later, eh?'

Desperate to make up for the past, she has one last go. 'It'll only take you a moment.' Grandad walks in, glancing at Danny. He can sense discord in the air. He has a nose for that sort of thing. 'Please Danny, I need to know if it fits.' She doesn't. What she wants from Danny is excitement, enthusiasm for the new life. Danny gives the labels a glance and delivers his verdict.

'It fits,' he grunts.

'What's the matter with you?' says Grandad. 'Your mother's spent all that money on you and you can't even try it on.'

Cathy feels something like a kick in her stomach. 'Dad, don't.'

But he does. 'No gratitude these days. There was a time in this country . . .'

'What you mean,' Danny snaps, 'is before people like me were here.'

'I mean exactly what I say,' Grandad retorts, sidestepping

46

the barbed comment. 'You should try the uniform on when your mother asks you.'

'I'll try it on when I feel like it,' says Danny and stamps out of the room.

'That boy's got an attitude,' says Dad, 'a real edge.'

Flushed with anger, Cathy brushes past him. Is this what she's brought Danny back to? 'He has now,' she says. 'Thanks to you.'

She follows Danny out into the backyard. 'Are you all right, love?'

He shrugs. 'I'm fine. I'll wear the uniform, but not because *he* says. He hates me.'

'Danny, he doesn't hate you.'

'Oh yes he does. I'm the wrong shade, aren't I?' With a touch of bitter humour he adds: 'I don't match the colour of the paintwork.'

'No, that's not true. He . . .'

Danny interrupts. 'Say he's not a racist. Go on, tell me he's not a stinking, smelly old bigot.'

Cathy wants to smile. Danny's acting like a little boy again, spitting out a string of insults to get his own back. 'He's stuck in his ways,' says Cathy. 'He finds it hard to accept new things.'

What am I doing? she thinks. It sounds as if I'm defending the old grouch.

'I'm an embarrassment, aren't I?' Danny asks. Then, with a mocking laugh. 'I'll tell you what I am: the black sheep of the family.'

There's no point in arguing with Danny. He's a young man now, a very bright young man, and he knows exactly how Grandad's mind works. Cathy looks over the yard wall. It's crumbling and badly in need of pointing. Beyond she can see the Edge, looking monstrous and dark in the fading light of late afternoon. The exchange of words has taken the shine off her optimism. 'Not quite the new life we wanted, is it?' she says.

Danny gives another shrug. Grandad's attitude obviously hurts, but Danny's pretty hard-boiled. He's had to be. After all, he survived Chris.

'We'll manage,' says Danny, his voice softening.

'Yes,' says Cathy, wondering what else is going on in

47

Danny's mind. 'We'll manage.' She rubs his back the way she did when he was little. 'We always do.'

Chris

Chris is managing too. He has no other choice. He has begun cooking himself meals. He has begun to clean and tidy. Sure, it's a bit of a guy flat, but it is presentable. No sense letting yourself go. But making the place habitable isn't enough to get his life back on an even keel. Everything is still off-kilter. Sometimes, as he walks around the flat, he feels as if he is becoming invisible, half a person. For three years he has seen himself through the eyes of Cathy, her brat too, to some extent. The fear he saw there was proof of his power, his manhood. Now, without his flinching audience, he is a shadow of his former self.

'Roll on Monday,' he says to the empty rooms.

Then I'll be on their trail. I'll have back what's mine.

Without Cathy he is only half a man, but soon she will be back, making him whole again.

'Soon Cathy, soon.'

He decides to make himself something to eat. That's right, a quick stir-fry will go some way to easing the gnawing void inside. He heads for the kitchen and trips over the loose corner of carpet. He'd forgotten all about it until now. Cursing he kicks it back into place and gets a hammer and some tacks. He kneels down and notices the yellowing newspaper underneath the carpet.

'What a cheapskate,' he says out loud. 'Lining it with old newspaper. As if I didn't give her enough money to pay for some decent underlay.'

He starts to read one of the headlines, but immediately loses interest. These local rags, with their WI meetings and flower shows. He pokes the newspaper back under the carpet with the hammer and tacks it back into place. There, that should keep it secure. He stands up and looks at his handiwork. That's the last time I trip over that. He smiles at the thought of it. Just imagine if I'd fallen and broken my neck on it. You'd love that, wouldn't you Cathy? Solve all your problems, wouldn't it, if old Chrissie had an accident. The way would be clear for you to take up your old life, but without me.

'Well, forget it, Cathy girl. Come Monday you'll have your old life back, all right. But I'll be right there in the middle of it. You don't get rid of me that easily. You're mine, Cathy.'

He emphasises his words by slamming the hammer into the door causing a small indentation.

'Mine!'

5

Danny

Danny finishes lacing up his trainers. 'Going for a run,' he calls.

'See you, Danny,' says Mum.

'Bye love,' says Gran.

But from Grandad, nothing. This alone gives Danny pause for thought. What does it mean? Is the old guy softening? Has he taken a long, hard look at himself? Could things actually be looking up? One thing's for sure, Grumbleguts's open hostility's gone, replaced by a kind of sadness. Danny doesn't understand it really. What's there for him to be sad about? As Danny sets foot outside the door he stumbles. He's tripped over somebody's leg. It's the lad next door. What's his name? Parker, that's it. All Danny knows is, Grandad's got some kind of downer on him.

'Sorry,' says Danny instinctively, even though he knows it wasn't his fault. He adds an ice-breaking smile.

Parker isn't alone. There are three of them in standard teen-issue baseball caps and nylon jackets. No protection against the cold, but 100 per cent proof against accusations of being a nerd.

'You living there?' asks Parker, nodding at number one.

There's something in his voice that sets alarm bells ringing in Danny's head. After three years living with Chris, he has learned that not all questions are innocent.

'Yes, it's my grandparents' house.' Danny registers the raised eyebrows and wonders where this is going.

'Old man Mangam kept you quiet.'

I bet he did, thinks Danny. I'm the black sheep.

'So how long are you staying?'

Danny resists the temptation to shoot back a defiant *What's it to you?* and shrugs. 'Maybe for good.'

Parker and his mates exchange glances. The alarm bells have been replaced by the prolonged wailing of an emergency service siren.

Danny feels more than a twinge of anxiety. 'Your name's Parker, isn't it?' he says in a second attempt to break the ice.

'That's right, Steven Parker. You?'

'Danny Mangam.'

There isn't a flicker of expression. No Hi Danny, no introductory banter, no warmth.

'I'll see you around then,' says Danny, with forced brightness. He turns and sets off on his run.

'Yes,' says Steven Parker. 'See you around.'

He says something else too, but Danny can't quite make it out. What he does hear is a loud guffaw from Steve's mates. That's another thing he's learned from his time with Chris, laughter can be a whole lot nastier than a shout or a yell. Danny has a feeling the mocking bray is meant for him. He feels it smack between his shoulder blades like a fist. He lengthens his stride. He isn't going to hang around to listen to the joke.

HARRY

He's been keeping an eye on the Parker boy. He's been half-expecting this. Harry feels something like guilt. He knows what your fancy college professors would say. Harry Mangam, Steven Parker, colour-prejudiced, the pair of them. Racists. Bigots. Shame on you, Harry Mangam. It's not true, Harry protests inside his head, indignation boiling out of him.

I'm not like the Parker boy, not by a long shot. Though they might hang from the one rail, they're not cut from the same cloth at all. Granted, Harry Mangam thinks you should stick with your own kind. He doesn't hold with all this mixing. You know what they say, the lion doesn't lie down with the lamb. He's never hidden his views either. That's how he was brought up, a true Brit and proud of it, and he doesn't see any reason to change. All these coffee-coloured children you see on the television. It's not the England he grew up in. They make him uncomfortable. Just like Danny makes him uncomfortable. But he wouldn't say anything. He wouldn't *do* anything. That's the different between him and the Parker boy. He has his opinions, does Harry Mangam, but that's all they are, opinions. Ask him what he thinks and he'll tell you. But he doesn't go round shouting his mouth off, and he doesn't cause trouble. He doesn't set out to hurt anybody, not a living soul. Not like Steven Parker. He's a bad lot, that boy. Forever bunking off school, always hanging round getting into trouble. That scratch on Harry's car, those broken roses, the chime bells that went missing the same night they were hung up, Harry knows the damage is down to Parker. He can't prove it, though. He's sly, is young Parker. A nasty piece of work. Harry knows what happened down at the Edgecliff Stores. It makes him shiver to think of it.

'You in there, Harry?' asks Joan.

'Yes.'

'What are you looking at?'

'Young Parker.'

'Oh, you're not going out to him again, are you?'

Harry shakes his head. 'No point. He'd only give me a mouthful of bad language.' He looks straight at Joan. 'I was just making sure he didn't say anything . . . to Danny.'

The word almost sticks in his throat, but there, he's said it. He's owned up to his grandson, acknowledged him. He might be bad blood, but Danny's *his* bad blood. Harry is beginning to understand that he is going to have to come to terms with the fact. Catherine's mistake isn't something you can brush under the carpet. The lad is under his roof. Harry has obligations.

Joan looks out at the three youths. Anxiety tugs at the lines round her eyes and mouth. 'You don't think they'll bother him, do you?'

Harry sighs. 'You never know. I wouldn't put anything past them, not after what happened at the Stores.'

Joan

The Stores.

Joan shudders at the thought of what happened there. Her mind goes back a few months. She remembers the dancing flames, the pall of smoke, the emergency sirens screaming over the moors. Suddenly, it's like her whole family is sitting in a rowing-boat and somebody heavy is standing on one side of it, threatening to pitch everybody in the water. She feels the fragile vessel of her life rocking and bucking, almost capsizing. No wonder Cathy stayed away so long. If this is what life on the Edge has to offer, this uncertainty, this menace, their dirty words and dirty minds, then maybe she should have kept her distance.

But I need them, thinks Joan, her heart crying. I need them so much. Life alone with Harry is bloodless, the same thing every single day. All they do, these two tired people, is plod through life, struggling to find a word to say to each other. Cathy and Danny have brought love back into her life, and no sad, stupid old man is going to drive it out again. No ignorant young thug is going to burn it out either.

Joan glances at Harry then out at Steven Parker. In different ways the same virus works away inside them. But I won't let it catch hold, thinks Joan, I won't let it ruin my new-found happiness.

There's hope in her now, and she refuses to let it be extinguished again.

Chris

'My round,' says Chris, heading for the bar.

Tony, his drinking partner, puts his hand over the pint glass. 'Not for me, Chris,' he says. 'Things to do. I've got to keep a clear head.'

Chris smiles. They kept a clear head this afternoon. He sits back down and feels the comforting pressure of a roll of bank notes. Some hourly rate, that was. Yes, they certainly did the business down the High Street.

'How's Cathy?'

A scowl comes across Chris's face.

'Something wrong?'

Chris weighs the options. Tell the truth and become a figure of fun, the guy who can't keep tabs on his woman, or just keep shtum? It's no contest. In his line of work, once you lose your reputation you're finished. There'll soon be a queue waiting to wipe their feet all over you and take over your turf.

'She's away at the moment,' he says flatly. 'Seeing family.'

It was the first thing to pop into his head, but it gives him pause for thought. That's right, she's got family. Did he ever meet them? No, of course not.

That's something he insists on with his women. Once you're with Chrissie Kane, you don't need any other life. He'll give you everything you need. You don't have a past.

Just the present, a present controlled by him. There's no trace of Cathy's family in the flat, either, no phone numbers, no photographs. He doesn't even know where they live. Somewhere up north, he's sure of that, but The North, that's a big place.

'I'd keep an eye on her, if I were you Chrissie boy.'

Chris's face drains of colour. 'What're you saying?'

It's Tony's turn to go white. It was only a joke, male banter. He doesn't want to antagonise Chris Kane. 'Nothing.' There's just a hint of a shake in his voice.

Chris Kane likes that. Reminds him who's in charge.

'Just complimenting you on your taste in women,' Tony says hurriedly. 'You know, *when you're in love with a beautiful woman.'*

Chris relaxes. No need to fly off the handle, he thinks. Tony meant nothing by it. But if he did . . . he'd be swallowing his own teeth by now.

'Anyway,' says Tony, obviously relieved to see Chris settling back in his chair. 'Got to be off. I'll give you a bell if anything else turns up.'

'You do that, Tony,' says Chris. 'See you.'

'See you.'

He watches Tony step out into the drumming rain then steeples his fingers under his chin. Family. That's where she'll be, all right, up north with her family. But doesn't she hate them, especially her old man? Chris wishes he'd paid more attention to her when she told him about her past. But there was no point, was there? What did he need with her past? He owned her present. And yet . . . if he just knew where Cathy was brought up. Bad mistake, Chrissie boy.

He watches the rain running down the window pane. He wants Cathy so much it hurts. If only he'd listened. If only.

Danny

His run takes him along the Edge again. He runs fluidly, his feet padding over the spongy earth with even-paced strides. His breathing is regular and steady. He is in the comfort zone. When he is running, things become clear. Down there, in the cramped terraced house, he has to watch his words. He has to make all sorts of concessions, taking care not to antagonise Grandad, or give too much away about their life back in London. His take on life becomes blurred, unfocused. Up on the Edge, with the wind whipping against his chest and face, all the complications drop away. He knows exactly what life is about right now. It is all about laying foundations for a new start here. Forget all that stuff about going back to London. Chris is in London. Terror is waiting for them there. No, they've closed the book on London. Bit by bit they have to build a new life here. He has a picture in his mind, sharp, defined, bereft of unnecessary detail. At this moment, it means just two things: find a way to live with old Grumbleguts and settle in at his new school.

'Doesn't sound too difficult.'

It doesn't, does it? Avoid treading on Grandad's toes, keep up his grades, keep his nose clean. All he has to do is become the invisible man for a few months. But life is never that easy. For a moment, the complications start to nibble away at the edge of the picture. Potential trouble spots, that's all they are, but they *are* there: Grandad, Steve Parker, and who knows what Edgecliff High has in store. Danny looks down at the T-shaped building and decides to take a closer look. He scrambles down the steep slope, accelerating all the time until he is pounding headlong down the gradient. It is reckless, but what the hell, he wants to be reckless. He wants to hurl himself headfirst down the Edge Cliff, challenge it to do its worst.

'Yaarrgh!'

He roars at the top of his voice as he hammers towards the ditch at the bottom of the slope. Danny Mangam: running machine! A few strides before the ground drops away into the polluted culvert he braces himself for his leap, feeling the power of his taut, lean body. He can do anything he wants. One, two, three steps, then he propels himself over the litter-strewn brook and lands with a satisfying thump at the other side. There, told you, Danny Mangam, star student, best athlete, top man. Even Chris Kane couldn't break me, so the Edge certainly won't.

Slowly recovering his breath, he jogs across the waste ground, a series of huge concrete oblongs that suggests a demolished factory, and arrives in front of the school. He takes in the details: the freshly painted sign 'Edgecliff High School' – opportunity for all – headteacher Mr R King; the bright, welcoming reception area; the display work visible from the road. It looks welcoming, even stimulating. It compares well with the peeling paintwork and dingy walls of his old school. A few more days, thinks Danny, a few more days and he will see if it lives up to its promise.

Having run his eyes over his new school, he doesn't feel like climbing back up to the Edge. Instead, he takes a moment or two to get his bearings and sets off in the direction of Cork Terrace. He has been running for five minutes, wondering if this is the quickest route, when he sees something up ahead, the burnt-out shell of a building. It is the first sign of dereliction he has seen around the estate. Drab and uniform as the housing is, it has so far been mercifully free of symptoms of urban blight. This smoke-blackened structure stands out, but what takes his eye is a spray-canned slogan that has been untouched by whatever blaze gutted the building. It is just two words but it hits him with all the force of a battering ram:

White Power.

6

HARRY

Harry doesn't sit down for breakfast. Instead, he stands by the toaster munching a round of toast. His jaw clicks rhythmically. He is acutely aware of the sound. It annoys Joan, always has. Some days everything annoys her. Everything about *him*. But Joan isn't the reason he is hanging round in the kitchen.

No, it's the boy. He has been cold and sullen for a few days now. A real chip on his shoulder, that lad. Just when he seemed to be showing a bit of respect, too. For a moment Harry wonders if it's got something to do with young Parker. He rejects the idea immediately. No sense making excuses for the boy. He's got his head full of nonsense he's brought up from London. Doesn't think small town folk are good enough. He's got an edge, that's the top and bottom of it. Thinks the world owes him a living.

'Don't you want to come to the table?' asks Joan.

Harry shakes his head stubbornly. 'I'm fine here, thank you very much.' And he carries on eating, listening to the clicking of his own jaw, wondering why it matters so damned much to her.

'You look very smart in your uniform,' says Joan, fawning over the boy as usual.

All he can do is grunt. There, that's what I mean about respect. He's been like that for days. Even worse than when he arrived.

Maybe something has happened. But what? 'Hadn't he better make a move?' asks Harry, glancing at the wall clock.

The boy looks up. His eyes are hard. I don't know why I bother, thinks Harry. I don't deserve a look like that just for keeping an eye on the time for him.

'It is getting on,' says Cathy. 'You don't want to be late on your first day, Danny.' The boy shoves his plate back and stands abruptly. He gives a scowl and marches out of the room without another word. 'Danny?' says Cathy. 'Is there something the matter? Danny?'

Harry watches him go, hears the door slam. Typical, he thinks. That is one angry young man. He wonders what sort of life they lived down in London for him to act like that. Cathy's probably let him do just as he likes. He's got an attitude all right.

An edge.

Danny

No sooner has Danny set foot outside the house than his temper starts to evaporate. He's been thinking about that slogan on the burnt-out building. *White Power*. Bet Grandad would agree with that. Like all the other rubbish he agrees with. Him and his *Daily Mail*. Or is it the *Express*? Stupid old muppet! It's been a struggle to bring himself to talk to old Grumbleguts since he saw that graffiti. He thinks like them, he thinks just like the bonehead racists who sprayed it on the wall. But there's no point dwelling on it now. Danny's got bigger fish to fry than old Grumbleguts. He's thinking about Steve Parker. Something has been building for days. Nothing Danny can put his finger on, no direct confrontation. But ever time he has left the house he's seen the looks, heard the snide remarks, the caustic laughter. In fact, Parker hasn't said a civil word to him since that first meeting. Danny feels something, a disturbance deep down inside. This isn't the promised land. Anything but.

He walks as far as the dual carriageway and jogs up the steps of the walkway that bridges the busy ring road. Knots of teenagers in the Edgecliff uniform are making their way to school around him. A few of them, especially the girls, cast curious glances in his direction. He can guess at the whispered discussions:

Who's that?

He's wearing our uniform.

New lad. Wonder what he's like.

Danny stares straight ahead. He knows better than to meet somebody's look when you don't know what they mean by it. Another lesson in life, courtesy of Chris Kane.

'Do you go to Edgecliff?' somebody says. It's a girl, bolder or more interested than the others.

Without turning towards the voice, Danny mouths a cautious reply. 'Yes, it's my first day.'

'You're not from round here, are you?' A second girl is speaking to him.

'No, I'm from London,' says Danny. It's not strictly true. He was born here, in this mockery of a promised land. In a way, he's as much part of the Edge as any of them.

'London! So what brings you to a dump like this?'

'My mum's from here. We're living with my grandparents.' He should say something like: *for now*, but he doesn't get the chance.

'What's your name?'

'Danny Mangam.'

'Mangam? Not old sourpuss Mangam?'

Danny grins. 'Sounds like him.'

'We used to go over your way sometimes,' says the first speaker, an attractive blonde girl. 'You can't even stand in the street talking without him coming out to complain. I'm Nikki by the way, Nikki Jones.'

'Tracey Hughes,' says her friend, a short brunette.

Danny gives her only a cursory glance. Nikki's the one who's getting his attention.

'What year are you in?' she asks. 'Eleven?'

'Yes.'

'Same as us,' says Tracey eagerly. 'You never know, we might be in the same class for some subjects.'

I hope so, thinks Danny, giving Nikki an interested look. I really do hope so.

Chris

He doesn't like this. It reminds him of when he was at school. Many's the hour he spent waiting outside the headteacher's room, watching a crack in the ceiling or listening to the gurgle of the central heating, wishing the time away until he could be out doing something less boring. School wasn't a happy experience for the young Chris Kane. Remedial classes for this, opportunity classes for that. He wasn't stupid or anything. He just didn't want to learn what they tried to teach him. All the opportunities that came his way arrived after he left. The streets, that was the only university where Chris studied. And he was an excellent student, he graduated with honours.

'Mr Kane?' That snooty secretary looks at him over her glasses. It reminds him of one of his old teachers. What was her name? No, it's gone. Not that he cares.

He's got no good reason to remember his schooldays. What wouldn't he give to wipe that superior look off her face! Mind you, the withered old bat would probably enjoy the attention.

'Mr Dickson will see you now.'

She ushers him into the headteacher's office. Chris sizes up the man on the other side of the desk. Fatboy, he thinks. Chris has nothing but contempt for lardy boys. He used to prey on them at school, just for being soft and pathetic. He got a kick from watching all that pasty flesh quiver with undisguised terror.

Fatboy.

He doesn't say it, of course, just rolls the thought round his mind. He wants information, he wants to find out where his family's cleared off to, so he's going to have to behave himself. He confines himself to a polite:

'Good morning, Mr Dickson.'

61

'Good morning, Mr Kane. I understand you wish to contact one of our ex-pupils.'

'That's right, I'm looking for Danny Mangam and his mum.'

Danny! The brat, that's what he ought to say. The little guttersnipe that hit me across the face with his bag. But still he controls his tongue.

'Danny Mangam,' says Mr Dickson. 'A good lad. Excellent student. Some sportsman too. A credit to the school. We were sorry to see him go.'

Chris detects something in Dickson's voice.

'So have you got the address or not?' asks Chris, rather too hurriedly.

'Mr Kane,' says Dickson, lacing his fingers on the desk in front of him. 'Allow me to be frank. I'm afraid I won't be able to help you in this matter.'

For a moment Chris stares back in disbelief. He was expecting so much of this meeting. It was supposed to set him on the road to getting Cathy back. He blinks uncertainly. In truth, he hasn't really taken in Dickson's words.

'Come again?'

You can't be knocking me back. I can almost touch Cathy's skin, smell her hair, feel her tears. She was going to get down on her knees, beg my forgiveness, and now you're telling me I can't have her!

'I had a meeting with Ms Mangam just before half-term,' says Dickson. 'I'm afraid she made her wishes quite clear. She asked me not to divulge her or Danny's whereabouts under any circumstances.'

Under any circumstances. Chris senses the conscious drama of the sentence. He stares across the desk. You're taking the . . .

'Do you understand what I'm saying, Mr Kane? I have to take the mother's wishes into account. I understand that you are not Danny's natural father.'

Still Chris stares, unable to believe what he's hearing. Are you trying to tell me it's no go? I've got all bunnied up for nothing? When he speaks, it is short and to the point:

'Listen, do I get the address or not?'

Dickson's flabby face registers unease. There is nervousness in his voice when he answers. 'Mr Kane, I can't.'

Chris's jaw juts angrily. 'Can't, or won't?'

'Mr Kane, I don't think there is anything to be gained . . .'

Chris leans across the desk. There's no need to hold back any more. 'Listen here, fatboy. I want that address.'

Dickson has gone pale, but the fatboy isn't without guts. 'Mr Kane,' he says, bracing himself for the angry response. 'I think you'd better leave.'

For a moment Chris thinks about going over the desk and sorting the dirtbag right there in his office. He even imagines dragging the fatboy out in front of his own students, making him grovel and beg for mercy in front of all those kids. Then he draws back. There are the police to think about, and getting arrested won't do his prospects of getting Cathy back any good.

'Think you're so clever, don't you? Think you can cover her tracks for her? Well, I'll find her, with or without you.'

Dickson just watches. He doesn't say a word. Chris doesn't speak either. He storms to the door and marches down the corridor. Behind him, Dickson breathes a sigh of relief.

Danny

He can't believe his luck. Not only is he in the same form as Nikki, he's in the same set for Maths and English. The way she flicks her hair, the way her lips draw back over even, white teeth, the way she turns her body towards him, it's obvious she likes him. At dinner time they eat together in the canteen. Tracey stages a strategic withdrawal and sits with some other girls. Danny quickly becomes aware of them watching him and Nikki, but he doesn't care. Even when they start giggling he stays cool. What the heck, they're only jealous.

'So how come you moved back to the Edge?' asks Nikki.

'Family stuff,' says Danny.

Chris Kane is the last thing he wants to talk about. It won't do his chances with Nikki much good. People don't like problems, or even people with problems. And until very recently Danny was a boy with a problem, a big one.

When he closes his eyes he can see his mother's feet scrambling over the carpet as she tries to get away from Chris's swinging fists, his thudding boots. He can hear her screams, smell her terror.

No, *family stuff* will do. It's neutral, normal.

'Don't give much away, do you Danny Mangam?'

Danny smiles. 'No.'

Nikki is about to say something else when her expression changes. Steve Parker has just walked in with his mates, the ones from Cork Terrace.

'Do you know him?' asks Danny, disturbed by the violence of her reaction.

Nikki nods. 'Everybody knows Steve Parker.'

'He lives at number three, next door to us.'

Nikki lowers her eyes, as if trying to shrink herself, make herself invisible. 'Yes, I know.'

'Well, well,' says Steve, making a beeline for their table. 'If it isn't the new boy on the block. Hello neighbour.' It's the most he's said in a couple of days.

'Hello Steve.'

Steve winks at his mates. 'Looks like our Danny is settling in. He's already introducing himself to the local talent.' Steve allows the tips of his fingers to brush Nikki's hair. Danny glances at Nikki. She's carefully avoiding making eye contact with Steve. But there's no disguising how she feels. When his hands touch her hair, she shudders.

'Don't Steve,' says Nikki. He laughs out loud, quite humourless. 'Please don't make trouble.'

'Now what does she think I'm going to do?' says Steve, spreading his arms.

He doesn't say another word, but he leaves an impression. It lingers long after he has gone. It reminds Danny of Chris.

Chris

He boots a bus shelter. Stupid school, stupid fatboy. Telling him he can't see Cathy. *His* Cathy. *His* woman! Hasn't Dickson ever been in love? Of course he hasn't. Too fat. What woman in her right mind would want to cuddle up to *that*?

A middle-aged man walks past with a dog on a lead. He stares.

'What are you looking at?' snaps Chris. The man hurries past. 'Stupid old . . .'

Chris rests his head on the bus shelter. Another lousy dead end. Love hurts, ain't that the truth? He hears the school bell. Mid-morning break. He sees the uniformed kids spill out on to the yard and form knots of friends. They're enjoying one another's company. They're not lonely. But he is. Without his Cathy every day feels hollow and sad. That's when it hits him. Of course! There's more than one way to skin a cat. So what that old man Dickson won't cough? That mate of Danny's, good old Abbie, he might. He wasn't very talkative last time, but with a bit of persuasion who knows? Fear loosens the tongue good style. Chris lights a cigarette and smiles.

See you soon, Abbie. We're going to have ourselves a little chat.

7.

Cathy

It's the question Cathy always knew he would ask. All those years in London and hardly a mention of his dad. Now, ten days after arriving on the Edge he's interrogating her.

'Where's my dad now?'

She's talked about Danny's father of course, explained that *it just didn't work out* or *I loved him once, but now it's over*. They were just lines from soaps or old Hollywood B-movies, but they kept Danny happy, especially when he was younger. Besides, they lived over two hundred miles away; three hours on the train. It's not like they were going to bump into Des in the street. Cathy meets her son's dark brown eyes. The expression in them is intelligent and searching. But there is a hint of accusation there too. I deserve it, thinks Cathy. All the things I've put him through. She thinks about trying to fob him off again, but he's not to be put off, not now that they're home, just three miles or so from Des's house.

'I don't know, Danny. He could even have moved away. It's been a long time.'

It's been a long time, all right, but she knows exactly where Des is. She served his brother in the café yesterday and they talked. Des is living in the same undistinguished terraced house she used to visit when she was – when she *thought* she was in love with him. She sees herself in his house, in his arms and wonders if this isn't another reason she came back.

Because she never really got Des out of her system. Am I really that feeble, she wonders. No, Des hasn't moved. He even works as a mechanic in the same garage, with one difference. He's the manager there now. Is he married? He was, even when she was seeing him, but it's over. Des's wife walked out as soon as she found out about Cathy, and the baby. Des hasn't remarried.

He's a free agent. Cathy smiles with just a hint of bitterness. Let's face it, he always was, even when he was wearing a wedding ring.

'I don't believe you,' says Danny.

She meets his gaze again. It's no use. He isn't a little boy any more. He has a right to know who his father is, maybe even to meet him if that's what he wants. Reluctantly, Cathy tells him what she knows. It doesn't take long.

'He wasn't around, was he?' Danny asks once he has digested the information. 'When I was born, I mean?'

'He was around,' says Cathy. 'He tried to be . . .'

She remembers the confrontation between Des and her father at the hospital. He tried to be around but that bitter old fool drove him away.

'Your grandad hated him. Then there was his wife. When she got wind of what had happened Des had to try to save his marriage.'

Talking to Danny has brought it all back, how afraid she was, how lonely. Mum was a rock. She was there for the birth. Without her . . . Cathy shakes her head. It was hard enough even with Mum. Goodness knows, Dad didn't come near her once. He was there to drive Des away, but he was never there for her. All he cared about was the shame, the things the neighbours said when his back was turned.

'And after?'

'No,' said Cathy. 'Des didn't exactly put up a fight when Dad chased him away. Des is . . .' Try as she might, she can't think ill of him. When she says his name a fondness creeps into her voice.

'He's what?'

'Des is out for what Des can get. He had a wife and kid. He didn't want a schoolgirl with a new baby getting in the way.'

67

'What happened to his wife? Did she take him back?'

Cathy has only just found out the full story herself. 'No, she left him. I wonder if Des even bothers to keep in touch with her, or his daughter.'

'He doesn't sound much of a man!'

Danny is full of contradictory feelings. He is angry with her but angry on her behalf too. When he was younger he thought she could do anything. He didn't need anyone else. She was everything for him. Now that he is older he loves her just as much, but he knows her weaknesses as well as her strengths. In a way he is loving her for what she could be, not what she is.

'When you put it that way,' Cathy says, 'just the bare facts, Des probably sounds pretty thoughtless. I suppose he is. But there's something really . . .'

She searches for the word. 'Sweet. I know he let me down, but I still think about him.'

'But how can you forgive him? The way he just deserted you.'

Cathy shrugs. 'If you met him, I think you'd understand.' The moment the words have left her lips, she knows she's made her mistake. Immediately Danny says:

'I want to, Mum. I want to meet him.'

Chris

Chris arrives back at the school a few minutes before the final bell, this time minus the suit. He is wearing jeans, a white tee-shirt and black leather bomber jacket.

It could be months before he puts the suit on again. He leans against the same bus shelter as he did after his fruitless meeting with fatboy Dickson, and lights up. The first pupils to leave are dressed in their own clothes. That'll be the sixth form, thinks Chris. They certainly look older. He stubs out his cigarette and saunters up to the gate. As far as he knows, it is the only exit. Unless they squeeze through a gap in the railings round the back. Chris smiles. That's what he'd do. There is a steady stream of kids in uniform now. He cranes to see if Abbie is among them. It isn't easy to spot one boy among so many, but he is pretty sure Abbie hasn't come past him yet.

There! No, too tall.

Maybe that one. No, that isn't him either.

Chris is starting to wonder whether Abbie's in detention, or at a club, or off sick when he spots him. He waits until Abbie is off the school premises before he approaches him.

'Hello Abbie. Remember me?'

Abbie's eyes widen and he looks around for an escape route. Oh, he remembers all right. For no other reason than to stop Abbie walking away Chris says: 'I'm Chris. Danny's dad.' Pushing your luck, aren't you Chrissie boy, he thinks, but it's his best chance of getting Abbie to talk.

'I know who you are,' says Abbie.

'So you won't mind telling me where he is.'

'I can't, Mr Kane. I mean, you're not Danny's dad, are you?'

Patience, thinks Chris. Softly softly.

'I'm the closest he's ever going to get,' says Chris.

They have attracted the attention of a pretty Asian girl. 'You all right, Abbie?' she asks.

'I'm fine,' says Abbie. With her arrival, he feels emboldened to stand up to Chris. 'This is him Ramila, the one Danny talked about.' Judging by Ramila's reaction Danny's told his friends quite a lot. Chris grinds his teeth. The boy's got a lot of nerve.

'Now I wonder what sort of stories young Danny's been spreading about me,' says Chris.

'All Danny's told us is the truth,' says Abbie, standing up for his friend.

'Know that, do you?' snaps Chris. Who's this bit of a kid to tell him he knows the truth? Chris knows the truth about what went on in the flat, and he wasn't the bad buy. 'Got X-ray vision, have you?' Chris demands. 'You can see into our flat, can you?'

'I don't need to,' says Abbie stubbornly. 'I've seen Danny's bruises.'

Chris's eyes flash angrily. Bruises! He's got a broken heart but he doesn't hear anybody crying on his behalf. 'OK,' he says, 'Let's cut the bull. I need to get in touch with Danny's mum. It's urgent.'

Abbie turns to go. 'You won't get it off me!'

'Won't I?' Chris moves fast, seizing Abbie's wrist. 'You need to learn some manners, Abbie boy, and maybe Chris Kane's the guy to teach you.'

'Leave him alone!' cries Ramila.

Chris doesn't even look at her. He's got no time to stand arguing the toss with the girlfriend. Instead he slips a hand inside Abbie's blazer.

'Let's see,' he says. 'I'm looking for an address book, a mobile, something with Danny's name on. Am I getting warm?'

'Get off me!' says Abbie. 'I don't know where he is.' The way he twists and squirms tells Chris he's on the right track. 'Don't come that with me,' says Chris, crushing Abbie's knuckles in an iron grip. 'You know, and you're going to tell me.'

'Never!'

Chris finds the mobile and checks the directory. Danny's name has been wiped. Very clever. 'Open the bag,' he orders, still putting pressure on Abbie's hand.

'Ramila!' cries Abbie desperately, 'Get help.'

Chris makes a grab for the girl, but she's too quick for him. He sees her running back towards the school.

'Fine,' he hisses. 'So we're going to do this the hard way, are we? I'd better hurry up then.'

Danny

Danny's had plenty to think about on his evening run: the things Mum told him about his father; the new school; the words he had with Grandad; most of all, Nikki. He feels a bit guilty. It isn't even a fortnight since he was planning to ask Ramila out.

But he's not going to see Ramila again, is he? No sense

crying over spilt milk. Or is that milk that's never even left the bottle? Whatever, it's time to move on. The thought of Nikki makes him run harder, faster. Soon he's bounding and skipping over the debris that litters the site of the demolished factory. He likes the way her eyes wrinkle when she smiles.

He likes the way she bites her lower lip when he looks at her. He likes *her*. He's still thinking about her when he turns into Cork Terrace.

And freezes.

It's Steve Parker. He's sitting on the wall of number one with his mates. Great! Just when I was happy too. Danny hesitates for a few moments, turning the alternatives over in his mind. He has just about settled on slipping unseen back round the corner when Steve calls his name.

'Hey, Danny boy. Got a minute? I'd like a word in your shell-like.'

Danny walks steadily towards him. He works on his expression. Not nervous. The likes of Steve Parker will seize on any sign of weakness. Not hostile either. There's no sense provoking him, especially when he's got back-up. No, nice and easy does it. Unsmiling, but relaxed.

'Taken a shine to our Nikki, have you?'

'Might have.' Ouch! Just a bit too cocky.

Steve stands up. 'Well, you can forget it, Danny boy. We don't want you making eyes at our women, got that?'

'*Your* women!' Danny starts to laugh. It sounds so corny. *Our* women indeed! He does it in spite of himself, he laughs right in Steve's face.

'You know what,' says Steve, giving Danny a push, 'I might just wipe that smile off your face, chocolate drop.'

And that's it. He's finally come out with it. *Chocolate drop.* Where does he get this stuff? Don't racists ever update their material?

'I'm not scared of you, Parker,' says Danny, heading for the front door. He trips over an outstretched leg, but avoids stumbling. He's not out of the woods yet, though. A fist jabs into his kidneys. Not hard enough to double him up, but certainly hard enough to cause him discomfort.

'Cut it out!'

'Why don't you make us?'

Danny is wondering what to do next when Grandad opens the door. 'Get inside, Danny,' he says. Before he closes the door Grandad looks straight at Steve Parker. 'And you can stay off my wall,' he says.

'What if I don't?' says Steve, sitting down demonstratively on Harry Mangam's wall.

Grandad closes the door. He hasn't answered Steve. Danny knows there's nothing he could have said.

Abbie

He's alone, alone with a madman, and he's scared. Chris has let go of his hand and is twisting his arm up his back.

'So where is it, Abbie boy? Where's Danny's address? Got it in a zipper pocket, have you?' With one hand he's applying pressure to the joint, with the other he is starting to go through the bag's contents.

'You won't find anything!' Abbie cries in defiance. 'I haven't got it.'

'You know where he is though, don't you?' says Chris, shoving the arm even higher up Abbie's back. The stabbing pain is almost unbearable, but Abbie carries on shouting his defiance.

'He's phoned me, that's all. I don't know where he is, and I wouldn't tell you if I did . . .' His voice breaks off. It feels like his arm is about to come clean out of its socket.

'But you've got a phone number.' Chris's mouth is close to Abbie's ear. 'It's in here, isn't it? The only directory that really matters.' He taps Abbie's temple. 'Stored away in your memory. Now . . .'

He turns up the pain, causing Abbie to gasp. '. . . Whisper it to me.'

Abbie murmurs something through the pain.

'What was that?'

'I said . . .'

'Yes, go on.' There's excitement in Chris's voice, excitement and menace.

'I said, drop dead.'

Chris slams Abbie against the bus shelter. 'Now that was very, very stupid.'

But just as Abbie is bracing himself for more pain he hears running footsteps. It's Ramila. She's brought Mr Dickson with her.

Chris

'Well, well,' says Chris. 'If it isn't fatboy Slim. Not exactly the Seventh Cavalry, are you? What are you planning to do, flab me to death?'

'No, Mr Kane,' says Dickson. 'I'm asking you to leave before the police arrive.' He holds up a mobile phone. 'The sergeant at the desk is still there if you'd like to speak to him.'

Chris's eyes flick to the display. It's the right number, sure enough. He's more than familiar with that particular seven-digit sequence.

'I know you're angry and upset, Mr Kane,' says Dickson, 'But there is nothing to be gained from intimidating a fifteen-year-old boy. You will only damage your own case.'

Very clever, thinks Chris, making out you've got my interests at heart. He steps away from Abbie. 'You want me to leave him alone? Fine, I'm stepping away.'

There is no point getting arrested. He's got form. The local filth would like nothing better than to pull him in over a petty assault. 'I'm leaving, fatboy,' he says, sauntering down the road as slowly as he dares. 'But this isn't over, not by a long chalk. I'll be talking to Danny, maybe sooner than you think.'

The moment he turns the corner and knows he is out of sight of the two teenagers and the headteacher, Chris breaks into a run. Spotting the approaching police car, he slips down an alley-way and on to some waste ground. It doesn't take much to give the Plod the slip. He turns the scene over in his mind. He sounded confident and strong in front of fatboy and the two kids but now that he's on his own he can't hide the pain any longer.

This is down to you, Cathy. Why did you leave me, why?

By the time he is halfway across the waste ground tears are spilling down his cheeks.

HARRY

He watches the boy unlacing his trainers.

The boy? What the hell am I talking about? This is my grandson. He can feel something changing inside him. Danny's presence is forcing him to take a long, hard look at himself. 'How long has this been going on with young Parker?' he asks.

Danny continues unlacing the trainers.

'Why?' he asks, 'What's it to you?'

'You're living under my roof, Danny. You're family.'

At the mention of family, Danny looks up. 'Family, am I?' he asks.

Harry is taken aback. 'What do you mean?'

'What I say. If I'm family, why give me the cold shoulder, Grandad? Don't you feel anything for me? I'm your *grandson*.'

Harry stares back. The word grandson bites into his flesh like a barb. He feels ashamed. There is more than a grain of truth in what Danny is saying. He tries to recover himself, clawing after lost ground. 'You're my blood, Danny.' My blood. That's right. Not bad blood. *My* blood.

'Yes, and you wish I wasn't, don't you?' Danny puts his trainers in the shoe rack and walks through to the kitchen where Joan and Cathy have been listening. Harry follows.

'Maybe we got off on the wrong foot, Danny,' he says.

'Wrong foot! Wrong skin is more like it, isn't it Grandad? Admit it, you're ashamed of me. You always have been.'

Harry looks at the defiant rage in his grandson and he wants to roll back the years, scour away the stubborn pride that stopped him acknowledging this young man. 'Danny, don't talk to me like that. I'm not your enemy. He's out there.'

Danny snorts.

Harry looks at Joan and Cathy for support.

'You'd better make your mind up, Dad,' says Cathy. 'Danny's right. We needed your support and you disowned us. You might not be kicking Danny like Steve Parker, or calling him filthy names to his face like Steve Parker, but you think the same way. I can still remember what you said about Des. Maybe you're half the reason it didn't work between us.'

Harry wants to fight back, to tell her the real reason it didn't work. That it just wasn't right. But it isn't the time for home truths. 'Cathy,' he says, 'what's done is done. I'm finding it hard. I admit it. If only you'd never gone out with that man . . .'

'His name's Des, Dad. He's got a name, you know.'

'Yes, and once he'd got what he wanted he was off.'

'Harry!' The cry has come from Joan.

'No Mum,' says Cathy. 'Dad's right. But he didn't turn against Des because he let me down. He hated him from the start, long before I got pregnant, and we all know why.'

Harry winces. This is all going wrong. He started out trying to build bridges and now they are all yelling at him. As if he's the bad guy in all this. 'I only did what I thought was best,' he protests.

'Is that right?' says Cathy. 'Well, all you did was drive us away. Make your mind up, Dad. Are you with us, or with the likes of Steve Parker?'

She doesn't give him chance to answer. Instead, she and Danny march into the living-room and sit staring at the television. Harry looks at Joan for support. She just turns away and starts washing the dishes.

Joan

Stupid man!

Stupid, stupid old man.

Joan washes the dishes and cries out inside. Why can't you see, Harry? Why can't you open your eyes and see what's right there in front of you? Cathy and Danny are your family. Look at them, just look with your eyes open for once. Look, and don't listen to the mean, nasty, destructive voices you've got in your head. Cathy made her mistake, but she's survived and with no help from us, either. And her son, our grandson, he's such a fine young man. Danny is intelligent, well-mannered and decent. Don't you get it, Harry? Even though we've done nothing to deserve it, we've got a family anyone would be proud of.

She heard him come into the room behind her. 'Did you have to?' she demands angrily.

'They didn't give me a chance,' says Harry.

'Didn't give *you* a chance!' Joan spins round. 'Didn't give you a chance, you old fool? When did you give *them* a chance? You drove Cathy away, Harry. You destroyed our family for fifteen years. Well, I don't want you doing it again. I won't allow you to do it again. If Danny is angry, it's because of the way you behave towards him. You're a spoiled, silly old man, Harry Mangam. You're either too stupid or too stubborn to do what you have to.'

Harry is standing in front of her with his mouth open like a codfish. This must be the most she has said to him in years.

'Joanie . . .'

'Don't you Joanie me. You get in that living-room and apologise. Do whatever you have to do, Harry. Grovel. Get down on your knees if you have to.'

She is out of breath. Her face is like a pink light bulb and she is holding her chest. 'I've got my family back,' she pants. 'I don't know why they came home, what they're running from . . .'

There. She's said it. She's known ever since that first afternoon. Cathy and Danny only came back to the Edge to get away from something. It's as plain as the nose on your face.

'. . . But you're not going to drive them away again. Lord knows, Harry, I haven't had much happiness . . .'

The shadow of pain crosses Harry's face. She knows she is hurting him, but she doesn't care. He's got to hear this.

'. . . And I'm not getting any younger. This is our last chance to be happy as a family. Don't you dare spoil it, Harry.'

Her voice rises into a strangled shriek of rage. 'Don't you dare!'

8

Danny

'Go Danny, go!'

It's Nikki's voice. Danny can see her up ahead, standing by the running track. She's jumping up and down, her blonde hair swinging. It's a week later, just seven days, but they are definitely an item.

'Go Danny!'

Then the whole group of girls around her is joining in, sounding like the audience of an American chat show: 'Go Danny, go Danny, go Danny.'

He has destroyed the rest of the cross-country field. Most of the way he kept up the pace chanting rhythmically under his breath: 'The promised land, the promised land, I'm gonna find the promised land.' And with each drumbeat fall of his feet he was stamping out the memory of Chris Kane.

The promised land . . . stamp out the mouth.

The promised land . . . stamp out the eyes.

The promised land . . . stamp out the fists, the feet, the face.

I'm gonna find the promised land.

What has given particular satisfaction is the ease with which he has left Craig Stafford, one of Parker's mates, struggling in his wake. Danny decides to put on a show, especially for Nikki, and he sprints for home.

'Go Danny, go Danny, go Danny.'

He crosses the finished line, but he doesn't stop there.

Out of sheer bravado, and for the benefit of Steve Parker who is hanging round at the edge of the small crowd of spectators, Danny drops to the ground and does ten press-ups. When he springs back to his feet, breathing heavily, but smiling, Nikki is right in front of him. Her eyes, a deep Mediterranean blue, are sparkling. Danny will keep this moment for days. He will warm himself with the welcome glow of acceptance.

'That was fantastic. Where did you learn to run like that?'

'I had a lot to run from,' says Danny. It's the kind of offhand comment he used to drop into conversations with Abbie or Ramila. He sees the confused frown on Nikki's face and wishes he hadn't said it.

'You left everybody else for dead,' says Nikki.

As if to reinforce the point, Craig Stafford labours across the line in third place. The PE teacher, Mr Court, jogs over to congratulate Danny.

'Impressive stuff,' he says. 'I take it you've done this before.'

Danny smiles. 'I've won a few races in my time.'

'Then how do you feel about winning a few more?'

'Sure, whatever.'

'There's an inter-schools competition next week. I've already put in a team, but judging by that performance, not one of them has as good a chance as you, Danny. Can I add your name to the teamsheet?'

'Yes, I'd like that.' Danny pulls up his shirt and wipes a few mud-spatters from his face.

'You only did that to show off your six-pack,' says Nikki, grinning.

Danny smiles. He knows he is fit and lean. It is a moment before he lets the shirt drop back down. 'Hey, nice girls don't notice that sort of thing.'

Steve and Craig are passing when he says it. Steve snorts and says: 'Who said she was a nice girl?'

Danny can't help it. He has to react. Only cowards walk away.

'Hey Parker, what's that supposed to mean?'

'What do you think?'

'I think,' says Danny hotly, 'That you need to be taught some manners.'

'Yes?' says Steve. 'And who's going to do it? You?'

Craig laughs and they walk towards the school building.

'That wasn't very wise,' says Nikki.

'I'm not scared of them,' says Danny.

Nikki smiles thinly, as if remembering something: 'Then maybe you should be.'

Chris

He has been in the shower, trying to wash away the humiliation he feels.

Everybody's taking the mickey, he thinks as he pads across the living-room floor with his towel wrapped round his waist. First Cathy, then Dickson. Pretty soon everyone will want a piece of him. It's something he's learned in life: if you're not on top of your enemy, then he's on top of you. Chris sits down heavily in an armchair and surfs the channels, looking for something worth watching. Eventually he settles for one of those lame talk shows. The perils of daytime TV. A strip at the bottom of the screen tells the viewers what it's about: *Men who beat women.*

'Oh, here we go,' he says. 'What about: *Women who lead men down the garden path*? It's obvious what's coming. A load of sob stories. But nobody tells the other side of the story. 'Nobody,' snorts Chris.

He listens to two of the women telling their stories then switches off the TV. Faces like the backs of buses, the pair of them. No wonder they get a slap.

'Typical,' he says. 'You never get the man's point of view.'

He gets up and goes to make himself something to eat. He feels a pricking sensation in his foot. One of the carpet tacks has worked itself loose and become embedded in the ball of his foot . . .

'Must do something about that,' he tells himself, extracting the tack and dropping it into the waste paper basket.

He makes a cheese sandwich and takes it back to his chair. Not knowing what else to do with his time, he switches the chat show back on and listens to a third woman's story. She breaks down halfway through.

'Oh, please,' says Chris mockingly.

That's all they ever do, he thinks. Turn on the old waterworks for a bit of sympathy. 'Well, you're not getting any from me.'

Nor will Cathy. That's two outstanding jobs, he thinks, glancing at the troublesome corner of carpet. The carpet and Cathy.

Danny

Danny raises his face to feel the splash of the showerhead on his face. He is thinking of Nikki. She's some girl. She must be to look that good in school uniform! She's a promised land all by herself. He finds himself smiling.

'What are you grinning at?' asks a voice.

Danny clears the soap from his eyes. It's Steve. Craig is by his side.

'Oh, it's you.'

'Think you're so clever, don't you?' asks Steve.

'If that's in comparison to you, then yes, I probably am.' Danny knows he isn't doing himself any favours by taking this line, but he doesn't care. He has had more than enough of Steve Parker. Steve and Craig take a step forward. They are fully dressed and there are two of them. Danny is naked and on his own. He feels vulnerable, but not vulnerable enough to back down.

'And you can cut the lip,' says Steve, obviously nettled by Danny's reply. 'This is the beautiful North, Mangam, the *white*, beautiful North. We don't need some London smartass trying to take over our school.'

81

He shoves Danny in the chest, forcing him back against the tiled wall. Danny immediately bounces back in more ways than one. He knows he doesn't have to take this. He can change things. He can make a difference. He remembers how he hit Chris across the face. He smiles at the thought of it, and the way he told Grandad a few home truths. Yes, Danny thinks, I can really shake things up round here.

'So what sort of smartass do you need?' asks Danny, eye-balling his tormentor. 'You certainly need something. Were you born thick, Steve, or do you have to practice?'

He turns off the shower and starts to towel himself down. His heart is pounding, but he tries to look nonchalant.

'We're going to teach you a lesson you won't forget in a hurry,' says Steve taking another step forward.

Danny acts quickly, grabbing Steve by the lapel and dragging him under the shower. While Steve is still trying to pull free, Danny turns on the shower, changing the setting to cold. It sprays all over Steve. The move is so sudden Steve is coughing and spluttering, totally paralysed by Danny's sheer audacity.

'What are you standing there for?' demands Steve, pulling free. 'Just get him, will you?' But before Craig can get involved, Mr Court arrives.

'Everything OK?' he asks. He is looking straight at Steve. 'Still here, Steve?' he asks. 'Would you like to discuss this further in my classroom?'

A soaked Steve Parker makes a hurried exit, followed by Craig.

HARRY

'You did what?' Harry has just overheard Danny's retelling of the incident.

Danny looks up from his tea. Harry sees impatience in the boy's eyes. At least it isn't the raw hostility to which he has been subjected for days. 'I dragged Steve into the showers. He needed cooling off.'

Harry glares at Joan. She's still laughing. She for one ought to know better. Danny and Cathy can plead ignorance, but not Joan. She was here when it happened. She knows what young Parker is capable of.

'Are you telling me you've just made a fool of Steve Parker?'

'He made a fool of himself,' says Danny light-heartedly. 'I gave him a helping hand, that's all.' Harry is biting his bottom lip. His head is full of the acrid smell of smoke, the reek of petrol fumes.

'What do you think you're laughing at, woman?' he demands, looking Joan right in the eye. 'Have you forgotten what happened to the Stores?'

'The Stores?' says Cathy. 'You mean the place that burned down?'

'The place that *somebody burned down*,' says Harry.

The smile has gone from Danny's face. He remembers the charred roof timbers, the blackened walls, the slogan: *White Power*. 'Is it the one on the way to school?' he asks. 'The one with the graffiti on the wall?'

Harry nods. Shame moves over him like a shadow. He remembers the things he said when the Ahmeds moved in, how he ranted about *their sort* buying up the corner shops and convenience stores. He even remembers young Parker nodding his agreement. But he didn't think they would . . . not that.

'What happened?' asks Cathy, anxiety creeping into her voice. 'What's it got to do with Danny and this Parker lad?'

'They did it,' says Harry. 'Parker and his cronies. They torched the place.'

'You don't know that,' protests Joan.

'Don't I?'

'Well, don't stop there,' says Danny. 'We want to know what happened, don't we Mum?'

Harry can see by the look on Cathy's face that she doesn't want to know. Not really. She would rather sweep it under the carpet, insulate her peace of mind in a cocoon of ignorance. Danny won't give her the opportunity. He demands the truth.

'The Ahmeds moved in a couple of years ago,' Harry explains. 'The trouble started almost immediately. Some local people took their business elsewhere.' He is aware of Joan looking at him. He feels uncomfortable. 'OK, so I was one of them, but I wasn't to know what would happen. It went too far.'

'Go on,' says Danny, his eyes narrowing.

'A gang of kids started hanging round, giving them lip. That was all it was at first. Then they started throwing things and running in and out of the shop, knocking things off the shelves. Most of it was just petty vandalism, but it got worse.'

He is aware of their eyes on him. Joan, Cathy, especially Danny, examining him as if he'd been one of the Ahmeds' tormentors, as if he threw the stones, or swept the packets and tins from the displays. But he wasn't, he didn't. He just spoke his mind, that's all. He didn't *do* anything, he wouldn't. Harry Mangam keeps his nose clean. He is a law-abiding citizen.

'Pretty soon, windows were getting broken,' he continues. 'Gangs of teenagers would be there until all hours throwing stones, scrawling graffiti. The Ahmeds couldn't get out. They had put their life savings into the Stores. They were stranded. They just had to put up with it.'

'Then they got burned out?'

Harry nods. 'It was a few months ago. The eldest daughter was alone in the flat above the shop that night . . .'

'She got killed!'

Harry shakes his head. He can feel Danny's eyes burning into him. 'No, thank God. But she had to be rescued by the Fire Brigade from an upstairs window. I genuinely think that whoever started the fire thought the Stores were empty. That doesn't excuse it. It could have turned to tragedy.' His voice trails off.

Joan has to finish the story. 'Most of the estate turned out to watch the fire,' she said. 'It was really unnatural, all those people and hardly a word was spoken. The family came to get Shaima. The crowd parted to let them through.' She glances at Harry. 'I don't think one of us could look them in the eye.'

'Did the police catch the ones who did it?' asks Cathy.

'No.'

'And you think it was Steve Parker?'

Joan and Harry exchange glances.

'He was there.'

'But how can you be sure?'

'Because,' says Harry, 'For days after he was sitting on that wall outside boasting about it.'

'Why didn't you tell somebody?' asks Cathy. 'Why didn't you phone the police?'

Danny stands up and walks out of the room. Harry follows him to the door.

'No,' says Cathy. 'Let him go.'

'It's not my fault,' says Harry. 'I didn't set fire to that shop.'

'No,' says Cathy, 'But every time you opened your mouth over the years, you and everybody else like you round here, you put the ideas into those kids' minds. Dad, they might have set the fire . . .'

She gives him a look which puts a sliver of ice in his heart. 'But you handed them the matches.'

9

Danny

Next morning he meets Nikki on the walkway. It is becoming a routine. Tracey is with them but she doesn't say much. She feels uncomfortable playing gooseberry. Nikki chatters away for a few minutes then the conversation falters.

'Something wrong?' she asks.

'I found out,' he says, 'about the Stores.'

Nikki and Tracey exchange glances. 'How do you mean?'

'I mean,' says Danny, 'I know Steve Parker torched it.'

Tracey's face drains of colour. 'I wouldn't go round saying that,' she exclaims.

'Why not? I'm not afraid of him.'

Nikki puts her hand on his arm. 'Danny, you shouldn't go round asking for trouble.'

'I'm not. I'm just telling the truth.'

'You don't know that,' says Tracey. 'Nobody knows who started the fire.'

'You've all got a pretty good idea though, haven't you?' The two girls lower their eyes. 'Go on then,' says Danny, a hardness entering his voice. 'Tell me he didn't do it.'

That exchange of looks again.

'There's something else, isn't there?' asks Danny.

'Don't be silly.' Nikki looks away.

'Nikki?'

'You may as well tell him,' says Tracey. 'He's bound to find out anyway.'

Danny feels a hard thump in his chest, like when you swig an ice-cold drink on a hot summer's day.

'I went out with Steve,' says Nikki, still not meeting Danny's eyes.

'Oh.'

Suddenly she is in a big hurry to explain. 'It didn't mean anything, Danny. A couple of dates, that's all.'

Danny puts a hand on her shoulder and backs her towards the railings at the end of the walkway. His dark eyes shine like obsidian. 'You went out with *him*.' He takes a gulp of air. This boy who hardly gets out of breath running distance can barely breathe. 'Knowing how he thinks.' He turns and starts to run. Nikki starts to follow, but Tracey grabs her arm.

'Let him go, Nik.'

Nikki shakes her off and shouts after him:

'Danny!'

Cathy

Later that morning Cathy walks over to old George and puts an apple turnover and a coffee in front of him. Really milky the way he likes it. Already she is getting to know the regulars, the ones who come in to eat, the ones who come in just to sit. The bakery shop doubles as a café and it is rarely empty.

'There you go, George,' says Cathy. 'Fifty pence change.'

'If I was forty years younger,' says George wistfully.

'If you were forty years younger you might just have yourself a date,' she says warmly. They both laugh and old George shuffles down the café to his usual seat right at the back where he can while away half an hour watching the other customers come and go. Cathy is enjoying her job. Just doing something like making old George laugh is worthwhile. For the first time in years she can look in the mirror and say: *I like me.* She is about to ask the manager if she can take her break now when she notices a tall, black man hovering in the doorway. This was always going to happen, but now that he is here Cathy feels exposed, a warrior whose every weapon, every item of armour has been stripped away.

'Des.'

'Hello, Cathy. Our Caryl said you were back.'

She calls through to the manager who is doing the books in the back room. 'Dave, I'm taking my break.' She wipes her hands and takes two mugs of coffee to a table. She smiles at old George then sits down facing Des. 'Long time,' she says.

'You're looking good, Cathy.'

She feels his eyes on her and she's a schoolgirl again. She twists a lock of hair and smiles in spite of herself. But she isn't a schoolgirl. 'I'm a single parent with a teenage son,' she says. That's right, you're a grown woman. You've taken hold of your life and that isn't going to change just because a man has walked back in uninvited.

'Still looking good.'

'I hear you're the manager now.'

'Yes, top gun in a run-down backstreet garage. I've really made it.'

Cathy doesn't feel sorry for him. In a way it's comforting that his dreams are as unfulfilled as hers. 'You haven't asked about Danny,' she says.

A vein pulses in Des's temple. I've made you feel uncomfortable, have I, thinks Cathy. Well, good.

'How is he?'

'He is an intelligent, handsome young man. He's been asking about you.'

The twitch again. 'What did you tell him?'

'I said that if he wants to meet you, it's his choice.'

Des sits back abruptly, as if bending before a strong wind. 'Do you think that's a good idea?'

'It doesn't matter what I think, Des, or you. Danny's got the right to make his own decisions.'

'Yes, but all the same . . .'

Cathy cuts him off. The schoolgirl definitely is history. There was a time when she would have gone along with anything he said. But she is a thirty-one year old woman. She has raised a child. She has been betrayed. She has been hurt. But there is a steel inside her now. Sure, she's let Danny down. But you get tired of guilt. Nobody's going to hurt her son ever again, not if she's got anything to do with it.

'Des, you're his father.'

'I know, and I wasn't there for him. I wasn't there for either of you. You've got to understand Cathy, I had a family . . .'

'Don't you dare make excuses!' snaps Cathy. Her words whipcrack through the air. Several customers look up. Old George gives a shake of his head. Cathy is aware that she is blushing. 'Look, I don't want anything from you Des, nor does Danny. I don't blame you for what you did. We were both young. It wasn't easy for either of us. But don't make excuses.' She cups her hands round the coffee mug as if trying to absorb its warmth. 'And don't shut Danny out. If he wants to see you, don't walk away.'

She looks at him thoughtfully. 'Why did you come anyway?'

Des shrugs. 'I couldn't stay away. We've got history, you and me.'

'No Des,' says Cathy. 'We *are* history. If you were thinking we could take up where we left off . . .'

She stands up. 'Well, it isn't going to happen.' She speaks softly. Her manner is controlled. Her days of hanging on the whim of a man are gone. I really do like me, she thinks. 'Look, I've got to get back.'

Actually, she still has five minutes left of her break but she doesn't want to continue the conversation. Des follows and pays for the coffees. 'There's no need,' says Cathy.

'Yes,' Des replies. 'I think there is.'

When he drops the coins into her palm she feels the touch of his fingers. There's no denying it. She still feels something for him.

In spite of everything.

Danny

Nikki catches up with Danny in the canteen. 'Do you mind if I join you?'

Danny looks up. 'Sorry about this morning,' he says.

'*You're* sorry?'

'That's right, I'm sorry.'

'You've no need to worry about Steve. It was nothing you know . . .'

'You don't have to explain.' What he means is: *I don't want you to explain*. To find out that she has had anything to do with Steve Parker, it is more than he can bear.

'I want to explain.'

Danny sees Steve and his mates at a table at the far end of the canteen. 'Can we go outside? I'm not hungry.'

Nikki follows the direction of his gaze and nods. Out in the yard they make their way to the railings. They can see the waste ground where the factory used to stand and, behind it, the Edge. The sun comes out from behind a bank of violet raincloud and illuminates the bleak hillside.

'It was a couple of months ago,' said Nikki. 'We went to the cinema once and hung around together outside the off-licence. It was nothing. You have to knock around with a few lads before you find one you really care about.'

Is that me? wonders Danny. That isn't what he asks: 'So why did you break up?'

Nikki laughs. 'Break up? There was nothing to break up. We were never really together. Danny, I didn't even kiss him.'

'So why the guilty looks?' He sees something in Nikki's face, a hooded look, an evasion. 'You and Tracey, you're keeping something from me.'

'Not daft, are you Danny?'

'So, what's the big secret?'

'The last time we went out, it was the night of the fire.' Danny's eyes flash. The obsidian stare. 'I thought we were

90

going to have a laugh. I knew he was a bit of a scally. I didn't think . . .'

'What?'

Nikki bites her bottom lip. 'He started coming out with it, all this racist stuff. Not just the sort of jokes you hear from other lads, soft stuff. This was hard, nasty. It scared me.'

'And . . . ?'

'And nothing. I told him I wasn't interested. I went home.'

Danny rubs his upper lip with a forefinger. 'That's it?'

'Not quite. He kept saying the same thing, over and over again. Something about my coming along to watch the fun. *The fun!* My dad came in from work later that evening and told me about the Stores. I put two and two together.'

She bends her head as if trying to put her face right in front of his, to read his expression. 'I knew you'd hate it.'

Danny smiles, a genuine smile. 'Yes, I hate it. I hate the thought of you going anywhere near that dirtbag. But you've done nothing to be ashamed of.'

'I feel ashamed that I ever had anything to do with him.'

'Nikki, you weren't to know.'

'So we're cool?'

Danny smiles. He wants to hold her, but they *are* in school. 'Yes, we're cool.'

Abbie

'Number unavailable,' he says. 'Again!'

Ramila shakes her head. 'Typical of Danny. He could never remember to charge his mobile.'

'But this is important. He's got to know that Chris is looking for them.'

Ramila smiles. 'I'm sure he already knows.'

'That man's scary,' says Abbie. 'I keep looking over my shoulder.'

'I don't blame you. He's obsessed. You don't think he could find them, do you?'

'Dunno. If Danny's mum's got any sense, she'll have covered their tracks well. I wouldn't take any chances with that psycho.' He takes out his mobile. 'I'll give it one more go.' He punches in the number. 'Nothing,' he says after a few moments. 'Danny, what are you playing at?'

Ramila smiles. 'He's probably having too much fun up there. He's forgotten all about us.'

Abbie drops the mobile into his school bag. 'Probably. Let's just hope he can forget about Chris Kane.'

10

HARRY

He feels the ground shifting beneath his feet. It used to be easy. The phrases tripped easily off his tongue. His England was under attack . . . more mosques than churches . . . you feel like a foreigner in your own country. But that was before Danny came. Now, nothing is easy any more. Nothing is clear-cut. This boy isn't just part of Harry's England, he is part of Harry's family, his blood. What's more, he isn't just an idea any more, a detail of the family's past. He is flesh and blood and he is here. He talks to you, demands attention from you. He occupies a space in your heart. And Harry has no answer to what Cathy and Danny said to him. He does feel shame over the Stores. He does wish he had made a stand. He does want to make his peace with the boy. That more than anything. He wants to make up for the last fifteen years. But how?

Maybe there is something he can do. Maybe this will do the trick. Harry steps out of his front door and looks up the road. It is quiet, just after two o'clock in the afternoon. The kids are all at school. No gangs sitting on the garden wall. No run-ins with Steve Parker. He likes this time of day, when you can have a break from all the racket. He likes the wind booming over the Edge, the keening seagulls that flash white and grey in the sunlight. He likes the way the street is almost empty of cars. It reminds him of the late Sixties when he started courting Joan.

93

Yes, it's nice at this time of day. No arguments about parking spaces, no slamming doors, no road ragers barking their abuse. He likes . . . emptiness.

But on this empty afternoon Harry Mangam is not just taking the air. This is no aimless saunter up the street. He is going to his car with a purpose. He is going to drive into town. There he will visit two shops, a DIY store and a sports shop. He has a list, the torn corner of a brown envelope.

On it he has scribbled the items, not so much because he might forget them, but as a declaration of war. Young Parker is cocky and getting cockier. He had something to do with the Stores, that's for certain. He has damaged Harry's property, the car, the roses, the wind chimes. But Harry's real concern is for his own flesh and blood, for Danny. Harry gets into his car and turns the key in the ignition. There is a darkness in these streets and it is coming closer, creeping into doorways, threatening to steal right into your home. He glances at the house and thinks:

An Englishman's home is his castle.

And Harry Mangam's castle is going to be safe, secure against invasion. There will be protection, and there will be self-defence. He scans the list: mortice lock, window locks, baseball bat. He will never sidestep a challenge ever again.

Come near me or mine, you young hooligan, thinks Harry, and you'll wish you hadn't.

Danny

He takes the phone off charge the moment he comes in from school. What's the point of having a mobile if you don't keep it powered up?

'That you, Danny?' asks Gran.

'Yes, it's me.'

He goes into the kitchen. She has made flapjacks. He isn't used to home cooking. Back in London they didn't even have cake tins, never mind bake anything of their own. Mum's idea of cooking was to pop a ready meal in the microwave.

'Have one if you like,' says Gran. 'They're still warm.'

'Oven fresh, eh?' says Danny.

He likes this, the smell of baking, somebody to fuss over you. Maybe he expected too much to begin with. What if the promised land can't be got all in one go? What if it's more like a jigsaw and you need to build it up one detail at a time? Danny feels that some of the pieces are starting to fall into place. There is Gran with her cakes and her unconditional love. There's Mum. She has always been true as steel, even when Chris seemed to be breaking her bit by wounded bit. There is Nikki. Too early to start talking about love, but there's something between them all right. Something special. Anything else? Well, there's the running. He is already an overnight sensation at Edgecliff High. Four pieces of the jigsaw in place. He doesn't know how many pieces there are altogether and he certainly can't see the whole picture, but there's an inkling, the hint of a promise. It's enough to be going on with. Danny is picking up the last crumbs of the flapjack with a moistened finger when his mobile rings.

'Yes? Oh, hi Abbie. It's great to hear from you.'

Abbie doesn't have time for small talk. He cuts to the chase and tells Danny about Chris and how old man Dickson stood up to him.

'Never thought I'd have a good word for Dicko,' says Abbie. 'But he really came through for us.'

'He's not so bad,' says Danny. 'In his own way he was always on the kids' side, you know.' Danny is aware of Gran. She appears to be finishing the washing up, but he is sure she is eavesdropping. He picks his words carefully. No sense worrying her.

'You don't sound too bothered,' says Abbie.

'I'm not,' says Danny. It's true. He isn't. Already the kicks and the beatings seem to belong to another time, another world inhabited by a different Danny. 'He doesn't know anything, Abbie. Mum made sure of that. I'm sure we'd have heard from him by now if he did.'

The conversation continues. Danny asks about Ramila, then thinks of Nikki and feels guilty. Abbie asks how things are going. Danny answers with a noncommittal: *Not so bad*.

'Who was that?' asks Gran when Danny rings off.

'Abbie, a mate from back home.' He can tell by her expression that Gran wants him to call number one, Cork Terrace his home.

'Do you miss London?' she asks.

Danny knows that there was enough of a delay between her question and his reply to give her pause for thought. Gran isn't stupid. She knows that something happened down there, something that made him and Mum move North.

'A bit,' he says. 'I miss my mates.'

'But you're making new friends here?'

He thinks of Nikki and Tracey, especially Nikki. In spite of himself, he thinks of Steve. 'Yes, I'm settling in.' He looks up at the Edge and thinks of the graffiti on a burned-out wall, not a quarter of a mile away.

White Power.

But he *is* settling in, he *is* going to make this place home, and nobody, not Grandad with his stupid, out-of-date ideas, and certainly not Steve Parker, is going to drive him away.

Cathy

'What's the matter with you?' She looks at herself in the bathroom mirror.

'What *is* the matter with you?'

Fancy letting him get under your skin again, all these years down the line. Des is no good. She knows that. If he was, he would have been there for her fifteen years ago. He wouldn't just have gone running back to his wife and child. His *other* child. But knowing what's good for you and feeling it, feeling it right down deep inside, are two completely different things. When Cathy saw Des walking into the café she felt it all, the butterflies, the legs like jelly, the breathlessness. Nobody else has ever made her feel that way, nobody. Even at the beginning, before Chris showed his true colours, there was never the same thrill. It's Des, she knows that, it has always been Des.

'You silly little fool, Cathy Mangam.' She scolds her reflection in the mirror. 'You silly, silly woman.'

That's right, woman. A woman of thirty-one, with a child too. She brushes her hair. She shakes her head. Wonderful taste in men you've got! Look at the record. One small-town Romeo, two losers and a psychopath. Way to go, girl! She unlocks the bathroom door and walks on to the landing. She almost bumps into her mother coming upstairs with some towels.

'Talking to yourself, love?' asks Joan, with a smile. 'First sign of madness, they say.'

Cathy sets a foot on the top stair, then pauses. 'Mum, why haven't you asked me why we came back?'

'None of my business,' says Joan. 'I thought if you wanted me to know, you'd tell me in your own good time.'

'I think it's time now,' says Cathy. They go into Cathy's room and push the door to. 'It's a man, Mum.'

She hangs her head. 'Story of my life, I suppose. The wrong man. First Des, now Chris.'

'You're not alone there,' says Joan. 'I thought I had my Prince Charming. Trouble is he turned out to be a frog.'

Cathy sees nothing but understanding in her mother's eyes and feels grateful to her for it. 'I met this man, Chris. There had been others, though none of them lasted long, but I thought he was the one. He seemed genuinely interested in Danny. Anyway, he moved in. It was great at first, then . . .'

'Yes?'

Cathy unburdens herself. She tells Joan everything: the possessiveness, the beatings, the terror. 'I didn't know how to get away,' says Cathy. 'He got me so I couldn't even think straight. He said he'd come after me, hurt me, hurt Danny. Mum, I've let him down.'

Joan takes her hand. 'No love, you haven't. One mistake. You shouldn't have to pay for it for the rest of your life.'

Cathy nods. 'You're right. You're exactly right, Mum, and I won't. It's never too late to put things right. I'll always be there for Danny.'

'You already are,' says Joan. 'After all, you did the right thing in the end. You got away.'

The look in her eyes says: *something I never managed*. For a few minutes neither of them speak.

Joan

She watches Harry working on the window locks. He's changed these last few days, become more like the man she once fell in love with. Before he became dried-up and disappointed. Before Prince Charming turned into a frog. Before Cathy . . . no, don't make excuses for the old fool. He's the one who refused to acknowledge his own grandson. He's the one who drove away their only child. He's the one who killed their love with his cruelty, his complete refusal to compromise. She hated him for that. She hated him because he broke up her family. She hated him because he condemned her to a life alone on the Edge.

'That'll do it,' he says. 'Let's see you get through this lot, Mr Burglar.'

Joan goes along with the charade. She knows it isn't a burglar he's trying to keep out. This is about the Parker boy and the sickness that is out there on the Edge. The hatred of those boys for anyone who looks different to them.

'Do you want a hot drink?' she asks. 'A nice cup of tea or maybe a mug of hot chocolate.' She thinks about telling him what Cathy's been through, then decides against it. He would only say: *I told you so*.

'Tea would be nice,' he says. He reaches out and touches her on the arm. She hesitates for a moment then remembers the years without Cathy and Danny.

'I'll boil the kettle,' she says. She can feel his eyes on her back, willing her to turn round, to show him the slightest affection. But she keeps on walking.

Danny

He is running tomorrow morning, representing his new school. More than that, representing his new life, telling the Edge that, no matter what happened at the Stores, no matter what has been said and done in the past, he is here to stay. Danny sits on the corner of the bed listening to the sound of conversation from downstairs. The promised land? Maybe. Even Grandad seems to be mellowing.

Since he and Mum gave old Grumbleguts the earbashing of a lifetime he's really been behaving himself. He's becoming a ghost in his own house, always fading to the back of the room, leaving the talk to everyone else. Weird thing, Danny is actually starting to feel sorry for him.

'Maybe I should go a bit easier on him,' he thinks.

Danny's door is open and he can just make out the noises that are drifting up from the street. Out of curiosity, he pads along the landing and slips into his grandparents room. It is the only one which looks down on the street. From the lace-curtained window, he can see Steve and his mates sitting on the wall. Not their own wall, of course, Grandad's. They're telling Harry Mangam that Cork Terrace, like the rest of the Edge, is their turf and there is nothing the old man can do about it. Well, maybe that's true, thinks Danny. But I'm not Grandad. I didn't grow up here and I'm not trapped in its way of thinking.

He can do something. He can stand up to them like he did in the school showers. He can show everybody that there's a different way of living. He can live without fear. Without fear, yes, that's it. He knows more about fear than anybody here. He sees Chris's face looming over him, the back of his hand swinging down. He knows about fear, all right. He lives with

99

it every day wondering if The Animal will somehow, by his predator's instinct, track them down.

'I learned from a master.'

But even the great fear that was Chris Kane can be overcome. Its spell was broken when he and Mum ran for the tube a month ago, it was broken when Abbie refused to give up the telephone number and old man Dickson took his stand in the street. So it will take more than threats from the likes of Steve Parker to put the frighteners on Danny. He is scared, very scared sometimes, but he hasn't been broken by it. He makes his way back to his own room and looks at the number he will wear on his running vest tomorrow.

He will run without fear and tell them all: I'm Danny Mangam, and I will make this my promised land. You watch me.

11

Chris

At first it was rage that motivated him, hot, raw, *exciting*. Yes, that's it exactly. By running away, Cathy set him a challenge. She lit the fuse of his anger. But once he had time to think about what Cathy had done, it was no longer an insult to him as a man. It was a thrill. Far from being humiliated, he was made keener, sharper, harder. Only . . . only he has been thwarted. The buzz is beginning to wear off. For the first few days Chris had options. The school, that Abbie boy, they were sources of information, signposts to the whereabouts of Cathy and her brat. He knew he would track them down. The trail was fresh. Now, a month after the bird has flown the nest, her scent is going stale in his nostrils. For the first time he is beginning to harbour real doubts. What if she has done it, what if she has outwitted Chrissie Kane? He will be a laughing stock. His reputation will be damaged, maybe beyond repair. A man who can't hang on to his woman is no kind of man at all. He paces the floor, racking his brains. There has to be something. Think, Chrissie boy. He starts tapping his forehead with the index fingers of both hands.

Focus.

Tap, tap tap. Concentrate.

Tap, tap, tap.

'Thi-i-i-i-ink!'

His voice rises to a crescendo, the shriek of a wounded

animal. She's done this to him. Cathy. She's the one who's hurt him, she's the one who's wounded him, who's taken what is his. She's stolen it all. His money, his heart, his manhood. She's thrown down the gauntlet. But he can't pick it up. This woman, this adversary, has fled the field.

That's what makes him so mad he could punch his fingers right into his own brain. She has won without a fight.

Danny

Danny scampers over the ground, jumping streams, bounding over tussocks of grass. Pit-pat go his running shoes. Swish-swash go his arms at his sides. It's a big field. He saw the coaches arriving just before the race. They came from as far as twenty miles away. It's a challenge all right, a big one. Over the first part of the course he has been content with keeping an even pace, getting over that early barrier where your heart pounds, where you struggle for breath and feel your legs dying under you. He has done what he had to, staying in touch with the leading group, keeping them in sight. Now he is picking up the pace, abandoning the jogtrot he set off with and starting to run.

Pit-pat. Swish-swash.

He races down a hill, going round tree stumps and rabbit holes. Who would have imagined that, just a couple of miles from the heart of the Edgecliff estate, you would be out in the open countryside. He thinks of the slogan sprayed on a burned-out building, the sick heart of the Edge and runs harder, as if pounding out his defiance.

With-out fear.

With-out fear.

Danny Man-gam's

with-out fear.

He has half run, half plunged down the slope and is on the heels of the leading group. He sees their misted breath rising in intermittent clouds. One or two of them have noticed him and are trying to outpace him, to burn him off. He imagines what they're thinking.

The cheek of this newcomer.

Southern wimp.

Most of all he thinks about the other stuff they might be thinking, about the colour of his skin, about what makes him different. He has noticed two other black runners, just two in a field of forty or more. They're both out of the frame. They fell back long ago. So it's down to Danny. He's the one who's got to use the race to scrub away the slogan, to make the Edge clean again.

With-out fear.

With-out fear.

The boy in front of him is beginning to tire, rocking and moving his head from side to side. He starts looking back. Danny knows that's the end of his race. Danny overhauls him. As he does so he glances at the fading runner's anguished face. Suddenly it is as if Danny is feeding off the boy's ebbing stamina. I'm a vampire, he thinks, a running vampire. The thought of it makes him smile. The next runner turns and frowns. Danny can read his mind.

What have you got to smile about?

Images flash before Danny's eyes, like the light that flickers between the trees.

Him and Mum free from hurt, free from pain.

Gran and her oven-fresh flapjacks.

Nikki with her blue eyes and strawberry-blonde hair.

Even Grandad coming round bit by bit.

Danny Mangam moves up the field. He has got a lot to smile about.

Chris

He carries on tapping at his forehead.

Tap, tap, tap. Concentrate.

Tap, tap, tap. Focus.

Tap, tap, tap. Think.

Then the shriek again. 'Cathy! Ca-theee!!'

The yell comes from within his raging heart. Fury, despair and blood-dark hatred surge up like a jet of searing steam.

'Ca-theee!!'

He wants her, wants her now. He wants her kneeling at his feet surrounded by the money she stole. He wants her begging for mercy. He wants her looking up at him, eyes wide with terror. He wants her cheeks glistening with tears. He wants her *broken*.

Danny

He is up there now, part of the leading group. It is from this half-dozen that the winner will emerge. The rest of the field have fallen away, unable to sustain the pace.

Without fear.

Without fear.

Danny Mangam's without fear.

And that is the way he is running. Without fear. He isn't even aware of the act of running any more, only the rhythm of his thoughts.

The promised land.

Without fear.

He is moving up through the leading group. Sixth, fifth . . .

The promised land.

Without fear.

Fourth, third . . . he is in sight of the finish now. Among the crowd he can see Mum, Nikki, Gran, yes, even old Grumble-guts has come out to cheer him on.

Second.

Almost there.

Chris

He won't let her win.

He won't, he can't let Cathy get one over on Chrissie Kane. He can't lose, not Chrissie Kane, not the predator. But how will he track her down? How will he find her?

'Cath-eee!!'

He sees her face, her laughing eyes. She's taunting him, waving the wad of money under his nose. This woman, this nothing, has fleeced *him*, the hard man, the guy with a rep, and she's laughing all the way to the bank. Who knows? Maybe she's even taken up with a new bloke, feathering her little nest with his hard-earned cash.

He looks around for something of hers. Anything. Just so long as it belongs to Cathy. But there's nothing left. He has destroyed it all, torn it, ripped it to shreds, smashed it to smithereens. With one final scream of rage he visualises her face against the opposite wall and flings himself, kicking and punching, against that laughing face. He smashes into the wall with his fists, his boots, even his head. He wants to see her kneeling, broken before him. But she's not here.

Utterly exhausted, he slides to the ground.

Danny

They enter the final straight side by side, arms pumping, legs keeping stride. Danny is aware of the other boy glancing at him, but he keeps his own eyes straight ahead, fixed on the finishing line. He tries to put in a final spurt, to burn off this one last opponent, but there's nothing left, not a single ounce of strength to draw upon. He is running on empty. He is reduced to a running machine, hanging on, refusing to let go, but unable to make the decisive break.

It's no good, he thinks, I'm going to lose.

Suddenly it's back, the fear, not of Chris, not of terror, just of losing, of falling short of the promised land. He can feel the jigsaw falling apart, the spaces between the pieces growing until there doesn't seem to be one iota of sense about his life. He tries to recover the confidence and hope he was feeling as he closed on the front runners.

Without fear.

Without fear.

Danny Mangam's . . .

. . . losing. It isn't much. Just half a stride. But he has definitely fallen behind.

He digs down, deep inside, calling on reserves of strength and courage he has never imagined, never mind uncovered. His muscles are screaming, the breath boiling up and scouring his lungs. He is level. It is his turn to look at the other boy.

You're stronger than me, thinks Danny. A better runner. But not a better man.

I . . .

will not . . .

be beaten.

He doesn't see anyone, not Mum, not Nikki, not his grandparents. There is just a blur of faces, the flashing by of the sky and the trees, and the boom of voices. Danny crosses the finishing line and bends double, gulping down air and planting his hands on his knees. He has never felt anything like this. The race has torn the insides out of him, left him half-dead with exhaustion and pain.

Suddenly he is being congratulated. Mum's there, Nikki too, and his grandparents. 'That was amazing, Danny.'

'Are you all right?'

'What a race!'

Mr Court has joined them. 'I've never seen anything like it. Well done, Danny!'

Well done. Does that mean . . . ?

'I won?'

'Yes, you won.'

'I beat him?'

'No, it was a dead heat. The first one we've ever had.'

Danny straightens up. The other boy is walking towards him, hand outstretched. 'I thought I had the beating of you,' he says. 'But you held on.' They shake hands. Danny looks into the other boy's eyes and realises that he isn't thinking in black and white. For him, it has been one boy against another, a test of character. Danny feels good that it's this way. They're not all like Steve Parker up here.

'You were stronger,' said Danny. 'But I wanted it more. Looks like we cancelled each other out. What's your name anyway?'

'Doyle, Alex Doyle.'

'Thanks Alex.'

'Thanks? For what?'

Danny shrugs. Alex just grins and makes his way back to his friends.

'What was that about?' asks Mum, watching Alex go.

Danny pulls a sweater over his head. 'Dunno.' But he does. It was about lots of things, about being a winner, about belonging, about being the best you can be. Most of all it was about living, really living.

Without fear.

12

Danny

He is flushed with excitement. He has run without fear. No, it is much more than that. He has begun to *live* without fear. He can feel the world turning under his feet. Things are changing. I knew it, he thinks. I knew I could make a difference. I've stood right in front of people's faces and said: Look at me.

Look at *me*.

And when they looked, not at the idea of Danny Mangam, but at the person he was, they started to change. They changed themselves.

Mum, who expected to see a little boy who needed her protection, sees a young man full of pride and power.

Nikki, who expected to see her boyfriend running, sees her boyfriend triumphant, metamorphosed.

Gran, who expected to see a little boy, sees her grandson on the threshold of manhood.

Yes, even Grandad sees a grandson he could be proud of. And it's down to me, thinks Danny. I can make a difference. I have made a difference. So he listens to the family's congratulations, because that's what they are beginning to be, a family. Maybe, for the first time in his life, it won't just be him and Mum against the world. Even when old Grumbleguts touches his arm and smiles his support, Danny doesn't flinch or shrink back. But Danny can see the regret in Grandad's eyes, the desire to make amends for fifteen wasted years, so he is willing to forgive. It isn't Danny alone, or even him and Mum who want to make the promised land, it is all four of them together.

'Do you want a lift home, Danny?' asks Grandad.

Danny glances at Nikki. 'If you don't mind,' he says quietly. 'I'd like to walk Nikki home.'

'We'll see you back home then,' says Grandad. There's a twinkle in his eyes, pride in his grandson, understanding for his feelings.

'Yes.' Danny watches Mum and his grandparents walking towards the car. He thinks for a moment or two then calls after them: 'And thanks for coming.'

Nikki slips her arm through his. 'Come on, Danny,' she says. 'Let's take that walk.'

Steve

'Come on, Craig,' he says. 'There they go.'

Craig nods and follows. They have been watching Danny ever since he drew level with the front runner. It was touch and go there for a minute or two. It looked like Danny would take a lift in old man Mangam's car and slip through the net. Steve cursed loudly when he saw his plan unravelling. But now it is back on track. The chocolate drop is slipping into the pan, and boy, he is going to sizzle. Yes, just watch him sizzle and melt.

'I can see the others,' says Craig as they climb to the top of the hill by the railway station.

'Give them a wave,' says Steve. 'Let them know we're on our way.'

Craig waves with both arms. The signal is returned by Keith Sparrow and Jamie Gorton. Operation Chocolate Drop is underway.

Danny

Danny can feel Nikki's thigh and hip against him. He steals a look at her, the full lips, the slightly upturned nose, the long, strawberry-blonde hair.

'Seen enough?' says Nikki. But she's not annoyed or confrontational. She says it gently, as if she is flattered by the attention.

'Never,' says Danny.

Nikki's expression changes. The smile slips away. She stops and takes his hands. Their faces move closer and they kiss. Danny's hands slip round her waist and he squeezes her, feeling her warmth against him.

'You kiss as well as you run,' she says.

He puts a finger on her lips. 'Don't say anything,' he tells her, his finger still on her lips, beginning to tease them open again. 'Just kiss me.'

He has wanted this so much. To be wanted, to be loved. To make a life for himself in his new home. Suddenly it is all falling into place, all the pieces of the jigsaw, all the parts of the dream coming together.

Steve

He feels a shudder of revulsion. Look at him, Steve thinks bitterly, the chocolate drop, with his hands all over my woman. That's still how he thinks of Nikki. His woman. It took him months to get her to go out with him and then, bang, she dumped him on their second date.

He doesn't know why. For crying out loud, he didn't even get one lousy kiss. Now that's bad enough. These things happen.

But for her to take up with the chocolate drop, for her to go for one of them, that's just too much to take. And just look at them. They can't keep their hands off each other. It's disgusting!

'Somebody ought to do something about it,' says Craig with a knowing look.

Steve grins. 'Somebody will.'

'Don't they make a lovely couple,' Craig sneers. 'If only they knew what they've got coming.' Steve slaps Craig on the back and they start to jog towards Danny and Nikki.

'Aw, ain't that sweet?' says Steve as Danny rests his forehead on Nikki's.

'So touching,' says Craig.

Steve starts to run faster. He whistles between his fingers to alert Keith and Jamie. 'Let's do it.'

Danny

At the shrill sound of Steve's whistle, Danny looks up, but Nikki immediately puts her fingers under his chin and draws him towards her. 'Hey, I haven't finished with you yet.'

Danny hears the sound of running feet, but he ignores it. What's a few scallies running past when Nikki is here with him? 'Hadn't I better get you home?' he says. 'It'll be going dark soon.'

Nikki glances at her watch. 'Yes, I suppose so. No sense upsetting my dad, the first time he gets to meet you.'

Danny feels a twinge of apprehension. So far, it's been a great day. Everything's been going his way.

He's climbed to the top of the world, but he hasn't forgotten the way some people on the Edge think. What if Nikki's dad's like that? What if he can't see the boy, only the colour of his skin?

Steve

'Stinking coppers!' says Steve, leaning his back against the wall and checking if the coast is clear.

They were almost on top of lover boy and his girly when the panda car came round the corner. Talk about timing! All the stupid coppers saw was a gang of lads running. They slowed right down and eyeballed the four lads. Well, it stands to reason, they couldn't hang around could they? Craig's got form for starters, a formal caution for TWOCing , driving away this old fart's car and torching it on the moor. Then there's the little matter of the Stores. Keith got pulled the next night and quizzed about it. It's obvious the coppers have got an idea who started the fire. They wouldn't have to squeeze too hard for somebody to cough. Steve spits on the floor. Even the coppers are falling in love with our dark brothers.

'So what do we do?' asks Keith. 'Knock it on the head for the night?'

'Are you kidding?' says Steve. 'We'll follow them for a few minutes, just follow them. You know, give the coppers enough time to get bored and clear off. Once we're sure they're not coming back, bam! We do Danny boy.'

PC Daniels

'Sparrow, you say, Dave?'

'That's right,' says PC Dave Lancashire. 'Nasty piece of work. Joyriding, vandalism. Rumours of a bit of housebreaking.'

'So what do you reckon they were up to?'

'Dunno, gang fight or something.'

PC Kate Daniels cranes her neck to look back as they take a

left at the mini-roundabout. 'You don't think it's got something to do with him, do you?'

She jerks a thumb in the direction of a tall, black man
standing on the street corner, not thirty yards from the four
youths. She clocks him and makes a mental note of his
appearance. Well built, looks like he works out. Slightly
balding, but otherwise well preserved for a man approaching
forty. Calf-length leather coat. Like *Angel*, the vampire with a
soul. She laughs.

'What's up?'

'That guy on the corner, the black angel.'

'What do you want to do?' says PC Lancashire. 'Go round
once more?'

'No,' says PC Daniels. 'We've scattered them. I don't think
they'll be getting up to anything else tonight.'

Danny

'Well,' Nikki tells him. 'Here we are.'

Danny glances nervously at the lighted living-room. He
remembers the potted biography Nikki gave him. Mum died
five years ago. Cancer. She lives with her dad and younger
brother. Dad's a civil servant. Brother's a pain.

'Do you think he'll be all right about us?'

Nikki frowns. 'What do you mean? I've had a couple of
boyfriends. He's cool with it.'

'No,' says Danny. 'I mean, will he be all right about *me*?'

Nikki frowns again, then smiles. 'Oh, the black thing.
Behave yourself, Danny Mangam. It might be a big deal to
Steve Parker and his mates. Not everybody on the Edge is like
them. We get this big reputation in the local rag. You know,
the estate from hell, KKK city. But it's way exaggerated. The
whole thing's down to a few families.'

She pauses. 'Of course, nobody's ever stood up to them.
Maybe we deserve the reputation just for that. All it needs is

for good people to look away, I suppose.' She reaches up and runs her fingers over Danny's face. 'It's no big deal for me, though. I fancy you rotten, if you want to know.'

Danny gives a low chuckle. He's purring like a cat at all the attention. 'Yes, it's mutual.'

They kiss.

'Anyway,' says Nikki. 'I want to show you off to my dad.' She unlocks the front door and calls down the hallway. 'Dad, I'm back.'

Danny hears a man's voice. 'Come in then, Nik, and shut that door. It's blowing a gale.'

'No, I've brought somebody to meet you.' Nikki's dad appears at the door.

'You're Nikki's *dad*!' gasps Danny.

'Here we go again!' The tall blond man looks about twenty, certainly not old enough to be the father of a teenage girl. Hardly old enough to shave!

'I know,' says Mr Jones. 'Everybody says it. I'm a real baby-face. But I assure you, I'm thirty-five years old. There's a birth certificate upstairs to prove it. What is it with you kids? Why do you expect everybody over thirty to be a worn-out old wrinkly?'

Danny smiles. Is this what he was worried about, Nikki's Peter Pan dad? 'I only meant . . .' Danny's mind goes blank. He isn't sure what he meant any more.

'It's OK,' says Mr Jones. 'I'm only trying to take a rise out of you. Anyway, are you coming in for a minute? I ought to get to know this wonderful Danny I've been hearing so much about.'

Danny glances at Nikki. *Wonderful* Danny! 'Can't now,' says Danny. 'Mum's expecting me home. Another time, yeah?'

Then I can show you just how wonderful I am!

'Sure, see you then.'

As Mr Jones vanishes back inside, Nikki gives Danny another kiss. 'See you Monday morning,' she says.

'Yes,' says Danny, warm and full inside. 'See you Monday.'

Steve

'There he goes now,' says Craig.

Steve has been crouching behind one of the neighbours' privet hedges. He peers over the top and watches Danny striding down the street. 'Look at him,' he says. 'Thinks he's cock of the estate. We'll show him.'

We is Steve, Craig and Jamie. At the sight of PC Daniels, Keith's bottle has gone and he's bolted off home. One more run in with the law and his old man will kill him. Still, three is plenty when it comes down to Operation Chocolate Drop.

'Craig, nip down that entry and circle round ahead of him.'

Craig nods and sets off at a jog.

'Jamie, you stick with me.'

It's Jamie's turn to nod.

'Not bottling it, are you? Not like Keith?'

Jamie shakes his head. He's a year younger than Steve and Craig and wants to win his spurs. 'I won't let you down, Steve.'

Steve smiles. Three on to one. Good odds. We're going to take you down, Danny boy.

Danny

For the first time, Danny knows something's wrong. Halfway down Nikki's road he was starting to smell a rat. Now he's sure of it, somebody is following him. That's not all. Out of the corner of his eye he saw somebody slipping down one of those alley-ways. He put it down to paranoia at first, but that was before he noticed the two shadows cast by the street light. Somebody else right down the end of the road. That's it then, there's four of them, and it doesn't take a university degree to work out who. Danny digs his hands deep in his pockets and carries on walking at a steady pace. It takes great concentration not to look round, but that would be a trigger. They would be bound to go for him. No, easy does it. For now, at least.

Without fear, without fear, Danny Mangam's without fear.

It sounded good during the race. Now that he's all alone and being stalked by four shadowy hunters it sounds utterly pathetic and stupid. Without fear? As if! He tries to gather his thoughts. The one who went down the alley, he's obviously meant to get ahead and cut off the retreat. The moment he makes his appearance, the other three will come running.

Then it's wham, bam, lights out.

Maybe if I run for it now, thinks Danny. I'm faster than any of them. It could just work.

But it's too late. Craig Stafford has just stepped out in front of him. He can hear running footsteps behind him. Running footsteps? Of course! Up by the railway station. That was them too. Something must have disturbed them. No such luck this time.

'Going somewhere?' says Craig.

Danny half turns so he has Craig, Steve and Jamie in sight at the same time. But where's the other one? Danny frowns. This looks bad.

'What's the matter?' asks Steve. 'Forgotten your running shoes this time?'

'Cut the chat,' says Danny defiantly. 'We both know what we're here for. If you're going to give me a kicking, let's get on with it.'

He's used to pain. He's used to taking defensive action and making the best of a bad job, concentrating on protecting his face, his stomach, the other vulnerable parts of his body. In Chris Kane he had a good teacher. The best. He braces himself for the first blow, but it never comes. Just as his tormentors move in a voice comes out of the shadows.

'What's going on here, lads?'

Danny looks up. The speaker is tall, six foot two, maybe three. Well built too. Broad shoulders, a muscular chest. The man has his hands in his pockets and his leather coat is hanging open to show off the powerful physique. He looks like he can handle himself. What's more, he's black.

'This has nothing to do with you,' says Steve.

'Yes,' says Craig. 'It's none of your business.'

'Really?' says the man. 'Well, I'm making it my business. Now clear off.' He moves quickly, grabbing Steve and swinging him round roughly. Steve looks startled and shaken. 'Now, like I said, clear off.'

Danny watches with relief as the trio retreats.

'Thanks a lot,' says Danny. 'Mr . . . ?'

The man gives a wry smile. 'Stupid of me,' says the man. 'Thinking you'd know who I am. I'm Des.' He holds out his hand awkwardly.

'Your dad.'

13

Danny

Danny is in shock. He stares at the face that is half in shadows, half illuminated by the street lamp. He tries to see himself in there somewhere.

'How did you . . . ? What are you doing here?' he asks. He is struggling to find the right words. He doesn't know how to feel.

'I came to watch you do the cross-country,' says Des. 'I noticed that gang of lads and decided to stick around for a while, just in case.'

'I didn't see you.' Danny realises how stupid he must sound. Until a few minutes ago, he didn't even know what Des looked like, so no wonder he didn't see him! Des doesn't seem to think he's stupid. He says simply:

'You weren't meant to.'

Danny frowns. 'I don't understand.'

'Cathy told me about the race. Very proud of you she is. But I don't think she would have been too pleased, me just turning up out of the blue. A bit late to play the doting dad, don't you think?' Des pauses. 'You do know she's seen me?'

'Yes,' says Danny. 'At the café. She told me.'

'And did she tell you she sent me away with a flea in the ear?'

For the first time, Danny smiles. 'Pretty much.'

'Your mum seemed to think you might pay me a visit sometime.'

Danny shrugs. He's been torn between curiosity and a desire

to punish the man who betrayed his mum. 'I might have. It's not like I've got any choice in the matter now though.'

It's Des's turn to smile. 'No. You don't mind me turning up, do you?'

Danny pulls a face. 'Are you kidding? They were going to batter me.'

Instinctively, Des looks up the street at the darkness into which the three boys fled. 'Did you know them, the ones who jumped you?'

Danny rolls his eyes. 'Oh yes.'

'So what was it about – that girl you were with?'

'Sort of.' Danny ponders for a moment, then corrects himself. 'No, it isn't about Nikki. It's about me.'

'You?'

'The colour of my skin. They fancy themselves as sort of local KKK. You heard about the Stores?'

'The convenience store, the one that got burned down?'

Danny nods. 'I'm pretty sure that was down to them. They definitely know something.'

Des doesn't seem surprised. 'The Edge has got a bit of a name for that sort of thing,' he says. 'A couple of black families moved up there from my end of town a few years ago. They soon moved back.'

'Aggro, you mean?'

'A bit. Mess through the letter box, the odd scrawl of graffiti. Nothing too heavy. Mostly it was just a feeling their faces didn't fit. You'd know all about that, of course. Your grandad . . .'

'Grandad?'

'Well, he isn't exactly a member of the Nelson Mandela Appreciation Society, is he? He nearly had a fit when he found out I was knocking round with his daughter.'

Curiously, Danny finds himself defending old Grumbleguts. 'He's coming round.'

'Really?' says Des. 'Can't imagine Harry Mangam mellowing. He never took to me.'

Danny's face tightens. The way he looks at it, there doesn't seem much to choose between them: a stubborn, prejudiced old man and a father who walks away from his child. 'Maybe you didn't give him much cause.'

Des blinks rapidly, as if his eyes are stinging. Danny's surprised that somebody he has always thought of as completely heartless should react so dramatically. 'I asked for that, I suppose,' says Des, finally recovering himself. 'You probably think I'm a real lowlife for what I did to your mum.'

Danny meets Des's gaze unflinchingly. Living with Chris has given him a hardness, an edge. 'You said it, not me.'

They stand silently, neither one of them quite sure what to say next.

'Do you want me to walk back with you?' asks Des.

Danny shakes his head. 'They're gone.'

'Yes, but you could still bump into them.'

'I don't need a bodyguard,' says Danny. 'I can fight my own battles.'

Des greets his words with a raised eyebrow.

'I've got to live on the same street as them,' says Danny. 'There's no point my trying to hide behind somebody else. I've got to sort this out my way.'

'You sure?'

Danny meets Des's gaze. You're here now, he thinks, but will you be around tomorrow? 'Yes, quite sure.' Danny starts to walk towards the Edge, an inky iceberg rising behind the terraced houses. Des calls after him.

'Hey Danny, you could still pay me that visit.'

Danny's heart skips a beat. He's imagined this meeting so many times over the years. A father, an image of the man he will be one day. He isn't sure whether to let hope in.

'You never know,' he says without turning round. 'I might just take you up on that.'

Cathy

'You're sure you're all right?' she asks anxiously.

She is angry with herself for bringing him here, to the Edge. You selfish fool, she tells herself, dragging Danny back here just because you decided to go running to your mum, expecting her to put everything right. You closed your eyes, hoping it would have changed. Fat chance! Cathy knows how this place thinks, she knows the sickness that dwells in its heart. Goodness knows, it turned on her just for falling in love with a black man. What's it got in store for her son? How could I, she asks herself. How could I expose my own son to danger like this? Then she remembers Chris. She seems to be making a habit of it, exposing Danny to danger.

'They didn't hurt you?'

'No,' says Danny, 'It was nothing.'

Cathy sees her father hanging round in the doorway. He has just been told what's happened. Cathy wants to drag him into the room, to show him what his stupid ideas lead to, a boy nearly beaten up because of the colour of his skin. She wants to confront him and every stupid racist bigot in the whole country. You won't hurt my son, she thinks, any of you. Anybody thinks they are going to touch Danny will have to go through me. She glares at Harry and he turns away.

Danny picks up on it. 'I can handle it, you know. I'm going to have to.'

'Well, you're not going to handle it on your own,' says Harry Mangam. 'I've a good mind to go round next door right now and have it out with them.'

Cathy is about to say something when Danny surprises her by speaking first and in a way she didn't expect.

'Don't, Grandad. You could get more than you bargained for. They won't take any notice of you anyway.'

'Maybe not, but it'll make me feel better.'

'It's not about you though, is it?' says Danny coolly. 'It's about me and Steve Parker. We're going to have to sort it out between us.'

'No,' says Cathy. 'No way. I'll have a word with somebody. What if you can't sort it out on your own? This isn't just a bit of playground bullying. Remember what they've done. We've all got a pretty good idea what they're capable of.'

'Yes,' says Danny, 'And I've a good idea what I'm capable of.'

'And what's that?' asks Cathy. 'Getting yourself battered to a pulp? We could talk to the police. Don't be too proud to ask for help. If Des hadn't shown up when he did . . .'

Her father's head snaps round. 'What did you say?'

Cathy flinches at his reaction, but she stands her ground. 'Des saved Danny from a beating. It seems he showed up at the cross-country. He knew something was wrong, so he hung around.'

Danny feels the old man's hard eyes turn on him. 'Is this true?'

'Yes Grandad,' says Danny, unfazed by the bullying tone. 'It's true.'

Cathy sees the familiar look in her father's face, the writhing humiliation and hatred. Fifteen years on and his hatred of Des burns brighter than ever. 'Dad, don't start.'

He looks first at Danny, then at her. 'You can't be thinking of letting him into Danny's life. Not after what he did.'

Before Cathy can say a word, Danny interrupts. He speaks quietly, but firmly. 'Don't say any more, Grandad. My dad's done things he shouldn't . . .'

'Too right!'

'But so have you.' He plants himself in front of his grandfather. 'Don't you get on your high horse. Just don't you dare. You drove my mum away when she needed you.'

His grandfather's eyes slide away from direct contact. Cathy sees the shame.

'You know what?' Danny continues, 'You're pretty alike in a lot of ways.'

Harry Mangam's face is beyond red. It's a kind of bulging, thick-veined purple. Cathy finds it funny. But she's far too worried to laugh out loud. Anxiety lodges in her chest like she's been punched. Unaware of what she is thinking, Danny plods on:

'Neither one of you wanted to know us for fifteen years, did you?' He says it simply, without anger. His closing sentence is the killer. 'But people can change, can't they? I mean, you have.'

A moment's hesitation, then the correction: 'You're starting to.'

It's about the first positive thing he has said to the old man since he arrived on his doorstep. Cathy sees the dark rage in her father's face, then the confusion as he struggles with his feelings. There is fury, love and self-pity in equal measure. But Danny has done something she has never managed. He has silenced her father. She tries to remember how Danny managed to punch a hole in that righteous anger. Danny has certainly brought him down to earth with a bump. Finally, the old man walks out of the room leaving her and Danny on their own. Cathy wants to say something to Danny. She tries to find the right words, but in the end she settles for squeezing his arm gently.

Just to let him know he's not alone.

Chris

Chris is with Tony and that girlfriend of his, Gillian. They've been out drinking and they're all the worse for wear. Their feet are dragging and they stagger into the newspaper stand outside the tube.

'Why don't you come back to mine?' says Chris.

'I don't know,' says Gillian doubtfully.

Chris glares at her. Stuck up as they come, that Gillian. Horsey type. He wonders how a bit of rough trade like Tony got himself hooked up with this high class bit of fluff.

'Go on, just for an hour. Keep a lonely guy company. I've got plenty of booze.'

Gillian's still reluctant.

'Just a couple of cans,' says Chris.

'How's about it?' says Tony. 'The night's young.'

Gillian finally gives in. Chris smiles. She's scared of him. He likes that in a woman. Nothing like the flame of fear to warm the babes, to make them malleable.

The three of them virtually fall through the door and collapse on to the tattered couch giggling helplessly. Chris wishes Cathy was here. He feels like a spare part without a woman of his own.

'I'll get those bottles,' he says.

He is swaying as he comes back in. He lodges a bottle between his knees and struggles to uncork it. Gillian and Tony start laughing at his antics. Chris joins in. All of a sudden the cork pops out. Chris lunges forward and the bottle slips from his grasp. It falls to the floor and starts to glug onto the carpet. The red stain spreads rapidly. Like blood. Cursing loudly, Chris falls to his knees and starts dabbing at the carpet with his handkerchief.

'Shouldn't you pick the bottle up first?' asks Gillian. 'The wine's still coming out.'

Chris grunts and stands the bottle up. Toffee-nosed cow! What's she got to interfere for?

'Look at the state of the carpet,' he says, cursing. 'That'll never come out.' He sits on the floor, feet splayed out in front of him like a toddler staring at a mishap. Then his face sets. 'You know what?' he says. 'I'm going to get myself a new carpet. This piece of rubbish just brings back bad memories.'

Tony and Gillian exchange glances. He has finally owned up about Cathy's disappearance. He has spent half the night alternately bad-mouthing her and saying in graphic detail what he'd like to do to her. The violence of his language has really got to Gillian. She was on the verge of walking out of the pub a couple of times.

'Move that couch,' he slurs. 'I'm pulling it up right now. Make a fresh start. Out with the old . . .' He rips up a corner of the carpet, sending tacks pinging across the room. 'In with the new.'

He is like a dog pulling on a piece of rag, bent forward with his legs spread, yanking at the edge of carpet. 'Stupid, cheap market-bought rubbish,' he says. 'Cheap, like the one who got it.' Suddenly he loses his grip and falls back, banging his head on the far wall.

'You all right?' asks Tony.

'Yes,' says Chris, rubbing the back of his head. 'It'll take more than a bump on the noggin to hurt Chrissie Kane.'

Then he pulls up short. He sees the yellowing newspaper that has been acting as underlay. Frowning, he picks up a double-page spread, one that hasn't been splashed by wine. He says the name out loud.

'Something wrong?' asks Tony.

Chris ignores him. He is examining the newspaper. His mind is clearing fast, made acute and focused by the unfamiliar layout. He snatches the section of newspaper. He only ever buys the local rag. This can only mean one thing. The paper belongs to *her*. It's a compass needle pointing towards Cathy!

'Let me see.' He runs his eyes over the pages and smiles a thin, hard smile. Of course, he's seen this before. He saw, but he didn't *look*. He didn't grasp its significance.

'Gotcha.'

'Are you all right?' asks Tony. Now Gillian isn't the only one who is finding Chris's behaviour unsettling.

'Get out,' says Chris, his voice low and intent.

'What?'

Chris's voice is like a balled-up fist. 'Get out. Get the hell out of my flat!'

Tony and Gillian start to leave. 'That's it, clear out. I don't need you. I don't need anybody.'

But he does. He needs Cathy. Tony hesitates at the door, thinking about saying goodnight but there is a menace in Chris's eyes. The shutters have come down. Whatever is going on in Chris's mind, it is closed off behind a barrier of steel. The moment the door closes, Chris stands up and walks over to the drawer from which Cathy took his money. He rummages for a moment then produces a road atlas. He runs a finger down the index, then flicks through the pages until he finds the one he wants.

'So this is where you've been hiding yourself, Cathy girl,' he says, poring over the map. He picks up the phone and calls directory enquiries. He asks for Mangam, but the number is ex-directory. He hangs up without saying thank you. OK, so he'll have to do it the hard way. But what's a bit of legwork to a man like Chrissie Kane? He consults the road atlas again and sees the thick, blue line of the motorway. What will it take to get up there? Four hours, five max. I'm like a bulldog, Chris thinks, like a good old British bulldog. Once he gets his teeth into something he will never let go. Never! He gives a throaty, satisfied chuckle.

Just when he was on the verge of giving up, just when he'd resigned himself to starting over, she's fallen right into his lap. He closes the road atlas and gives a broad smile of triumph.

'Bingo!'

14

Danny

'Here's trouble,' says Nikki.

It's Monday morning, the first school day since the cross-country. The sight of Steve, Craig and Jamie walking towards him down the corridor is hardly unexpected, but unwelcome nevertheless. Tracey cuts herself loose and leaves Danny and Nikki to it.

'So who was the spade?' asks Steve. Danny hates that word, a racist insult from an earlier generation. But he's heard worse and doesn't plan to give Steve the satisfaction of seeing him react. 'I said . . .'

'I know what you said, Steve,' says Danny. 'The guy who nearly made you wet yourself was my dad.'

'Well well,' says Steve. 'Miracles will never cease. So you actually know who your dad is. You know what they say about women who go out with chocolate drops.'

'No,' says Danny, his face hardening. 'Maybe you'd like to tell me.'

Steve leans right into Danny, eyeballing him. 'Slags, the lot of them.'

Slags. The word ricochets through Danny, slamming into his spine. Nikki reaches for his arm but she's too late. Danny throws a right hand that snaps Steve's head back. Before Craig or Jamie can do a thing about it, Danny has hit him again, popping his skull into the display board behind him, making it rattle and boom. The huge crash echoes down the corridor. Danny views his handiwork with satisfaction. Blood is bubbling out of one of Steve's nostrils and there are flecks of it on his shirt. Steve's eyes are glassy but he hasn't gone down. It's only a matter of time before he clears his head and comes back, fists flailing.

And he's got backup in the shape of his two mates. Craig is the first to go for Danny. 'You've had it for that,' he says, swinging.

The first flashfire of rage has started to die. Danny's anger is colder now, hammer-hard. Nothing is instinctive any more. He wants his tormentors to choke on their own insults. He rolls away from Craig's punch and it barely brushes his cheek. But already Jamie is joining in. He cannons into Danny, throwing him off balance and jabbing an elbow into his ribs. Nikki gets a handful of Jamie's blazer and starts pulling him back. All the time she is screaming: 'Stop them, somebody!'

Steve is still trying to staunch the flow of blood and is in no shape to join in. Danny takes advantage of this to throw Craig up against the wall and kick out at Jamie. He knows he won't keep them off for long, but he's determined to give them a run for their money.

He sees Steve leaning forward, dropping heavy gobs of blood on the tiled floor. A dark red string trails from his nostrils. Steve's voice gurgles with hatred. 'Kill the . . .'

He doesn't get to finish. Mr Court has appeared at the end of the corridor. Danny spots Tracey. She couldn't have gone far. She's obviously seen what was coming and raised the alarm.

'What's going on here?' demands Mr Court. He sees his star runner still squaring up for a fight. 'Danny?' He looks concerned. Disappointed too. He steps in front of Danny. 'Just put your fists down, son.' Danny darts a look at Steve. His focus has been shaken. 'Do as I say,' says Mr Court. 'Please.'

Danny slowly lowers his fists.

'See what he's done, sir,' says Jamie. 'He hit Steve right in the face. For nothing.'

'That's right,' says Craig, hurriedly. 'Smacked him one, right out of the blue. He's probably broken his nose.'

'That's not true!' protests Nikki. 'Danny didn't start it. They did. It was three on to one. Just look at them, sir. You can see what was happening.' She is immediately shouted down. The three boys are spitting obscenities. Craig especially.

'Cut out the language, lad,' says Mr Court. When he has finally restored a semblance of order, he lowers his voice almost to a whisper. 'I think,' he says, glaring at Steve and his mates, 'that you all need to calm down. I will have to report an incident as serious as this to Mr King.'

The mention of the headteacher makes Nikki bite her lower lip, but it has little effect on the four boys. Steve has had more than his fair share of run-ins with authority and he has had two short-term exclusions. Craig has one to his name. Jamie has managed to steer clear of formal sanctions, mostly because he is rarely in school long enough to be disciplined. They wear their defiance as a badge of merit. It marks them out, the hard men of the school. As for Danny, he is staring at Steve with burning eyes. He wants to ram his filthy words back down his enemy's throat, no matter what it costs him in cuts and bruises later. Danny has started making a life for himself here on the Edge and nobody – especially not Steve Parker – is going to take it away from him.

Nobody.

Des

The man Steve Parker has just called *the spade* to Danny's face is checking the list of jobs at High Street Auto Repairs. Des flicks through the dockets. 'Have you done that service on the red Fiesta?' he asks John, a young mechanic.

'Just changing the oil.'

'OK, take your break when you're finished with that.'

He walks to the steel concertina doors and looks up the street. When he suggested that Danny might want to call on him, it was a gesture. Like promising to keep in touch with a school friend. Like telling an old flame you'll call. It's more than that now. He is hoping Danny will take him up on it. *He's my son.* Des watches a young mother walk by hand-in-hand with a bright-eyed three-year-old. He remembers his other child, his daughter Nina. She's sixteen now, doing well at school, on her way to university. Not that they have kept in touch. Her mother is so bitter. She's really poisoned Nina against him. Des laughs out loud then looks around to make sure none of the lads are looking. No, I've done that all by myself, he thinks. That's two kids' lives I've walked away from.

There is nobody in his life now. Sure, there have been women. Lady friends, his dear old mum calls them. But nobody special. Most nights he just goes home to his little terraced house and listens to Sam Cooke, Curtis Mayfield, Gil Scott Heron. It might not be his generation, but it's his music. Inherited from his own father along with the advice: women, love 'em and leave 'em. He knows what he thinks of that advice now. The same as he thinks of those stupid young boys who are giving Danny such a hard time. A recipe for unhappiness.

Abbie

At home time later that day, Abbie notices a black Ford Mondeo parked opposite the bus stop outside school. The driver is Chris Kane.

'Something wrong?' asks Ramila.

Abbie nods. 'Over there.'

Ramila's eyes take on a hooded look. 'Do you think we should tell Mr Dickson?'

Abbie doesn't take his eyes off Chris. 'I don't know.'

As it turns out, he doesn't need to do anything. Chris gives them a smile and drives off.

'What was all that about?' wonders Ramila out loud.

'I'm not sure,' says Abbie. 'But I think Danny ought to

know.' He punches his friend's number into the mobile. He gets *number unattainable*.

Danny

Danny can't take messages. He is sitting in the head's office with Mum.

'The reason I wanted to talk to you, Mrs Mangam,' Mr King is explaining, 'Is this: Danny is new to the school and I was wondering if he has been having any problems.' He reads a note on his clipboard. 'I notice that you live next door to Steven Parker. Is there some friction between them?'

'There has been a bit of bother,' says Mum. 'Maybe you'd like to explain, Danny.'

Danny just stares down at his shoes. He doesn't want to explain anything. There's nothing to explain. Some scumbag bad-mouths your mother, you do them. Some racist moron gives you verbal, you punish them. Simple as that. It's called rough justice.

'Steve Parker is a bad lot,' Mum says. 'He's involved in a racist gang. They burned down the Stores.'

Mr King immediately holds up his hands, palms outward. 'That's a serious allegation, Mrs Mangam. Do you have any evidence to support it?'

Mum hesitates, then shakes her head. She decides to confine herself to the facts, the bare bones. 'He has been goading Danny ever since we moved in.'

'And it is this goading which led to today's incident?'

Mum nods. 'Danny was defending himself . . . and me.'

'You?'

'Steve Parker was using offensive language about me. You know the sort of thing.'

Mr King nods. He does. 'Let me make this clear, Mrs Mangam,' he says. 'No matter what the verbal provocation, I can't have violence in my school. Let me also assure you that

131

we have never had any problems with racial prejudice at Edgecliff.'

Sure, thinks Danny, like you'd know if you had. Mr King continues, oblivious to Danny's thoughts.

'Danny has to learn that, if he has a grievance, he goes to his form teacher.'

'But surely,' says Mum, 'This is a clear case of racist bullying . . .'

'Mrs Mangam, there are procedures, clearly set out in the school prospectus.'

Danny raises his head and looks straight at Mr King. He was only standing up for himself and his mum and he is being made to feel like a criminal. Now Kingy is having a go at his mum. The resentment builds up inside him.

'I won't take any action on this occasion,' says Mr King.

'No action?' asks Danny, speaking for the first time. 'You mean you're going to let them off?'

'I mean,' says Mr King, 'I won't take any action against *you*.'

Danny rises to his feet. 'Me!'

'Danny,' says Mr King, waving him back down. 'You are the one who started the violence, remember. A member of staff had to take Steven to casualty.'

'Nothing trivial, I hope,' says Danny, cool, grim rage making a lump in his throat.

Mum looks pleadingly at him. She is torn between defending her son and *going through the proper channels*.

'You won't get anywhere with that attitude, Danny,' says Mr King. He laces his fingers together and rests his hands on the desk. 'Because this is the first incident of this kind, and because there was clearly provocation I will overlook it. But there must be no repetition. Do I make myself understood, Danny?'

Danny meets his gaze and looks straight back. His eyes burn like coals.

'I'll make sure Danny keeps out of trouble,' says Mum. 'But that's only the half of it, Mr King. I expect you to protect my son. If you do your job, he won't have to take matters into his own hands.'

With that, they leave the office.

MR KING

The headteacher parts the blinds with his index finger and watches the Mangams walking towards the school gates. He's got an edge, the Mangam boy. You can see where he gets it from too. The mother's no shrinking violet. She puts it all down to racism, of course. Typical. Who gave racism a moment's thought before he arrived? Nobody takes responsibility for their children these days. It's always somebody else's fault. It looks like Mrs Mangam's yet another of these high and mighty mums who try to tell you your job. She thinks the sun shines out of her son. It's about time she took off the rose-tinted glasses.

He's no angel. No, indeed. Young Mangam definitely needs watching. Mr King reads the names of the other boys involved: Steve Parker, Craig Stafford, Jamie Gorton. A real rogues' gallery. Now he has another name to add, Danny Mangam. He spots the school's multicultural policy on his bookshelf. It's all very well, thinks Mr King, all these fine words about equal opportunities. But what it all comes down to is boys with an edge, lads who act on impulse and resort to violence at the drop of a hat. Mr King is aware of a red ring circling a date in six weeks' time. There's an inspection in the offing so the last thing he needs his another trouble-maker. The first time any of them – Parker, Stafford, Gorton or Mangam – steps out of line they're for the high jump. Mr King watches the Mangams until they disappear out of sight. He calls to mind what he knows about their background: single parent, absentee father, abusive boyfriend. He sighs. He had his doubts when he took this boy but the glowing testimonial from his previous headteacher swayed him. Should have stuck with my gut instinct, he thinks.

Chris

He hits the motorway just before the rush hour, but it is already congested. For once, Chris doesn't care. No road rage tonight, just an inner contentment, the knowledge that he'll soon have what's rightfully his. He glances at the road atlas lying open on the passenger seat and smiles. He's got time, all the time in the world. Little does she know it, but Cathy is a sitting duck up there in her little northern hide-out.

'I'm coming to get you,' says Chris out loud in a sing-song voice. 'Hear that, Cathy girl? The big, bad wolf is on his way. I will huff and I will puff and I will blow your house down.'

He chuckles to himself. The big, bad wolf. Yes, that's very good. He imagines Cathy cowering in Daddy's house with the rest of the little piggies. He imagines her tears. He imagines her pleading voice:

Not by the hair on my chinny, chin, chin.

Chris laughs out loud. 'Wolfie's on his way,' he says, 'A-woooo!'

There is a little boy looking at Chris from the window of a car in the inside lane. Chris pulls a funny face and makes the kid laugh. Once more he says it: 'Wolfie's on his way.'

Then the battle-cry: 'A-wooooo!'

Danny

'You could have been a bit more polite,' Mum says. 'I'm sure Mr King was only trying to help.'

'So why didn't he have Parker's parents in?' Danny asks. 'Or Stafford's, or Gorton's? Why just me?'

'He probably thinks there isn't much point seeing their families. I don't think they care.'

Danny shakes his head. 'He thinks I started it.'

'Danny, you're wrong. When he phoned me, he said he just wanted to touch base with me, make sure this didn't turn into anything serious. He's got your interests at heart.'

Danny listens to the gobbledy-gook. *Interests at heart . . . touch base . . .*

What's that supposed to mean? Danny knows the agenda, even if Mum doesn't. He's been picked out, highlighted as a troublemaker. He saw it in Mr King's eyes. From now on, no matter what Steve and his gang get up to, no matter how much they lean on him or wind him up, Danny's the one who will be watched. He's the one whose behaviour will be noted.

'You did listen to what he said, didn't you?'

'Which bit?'

'That you mustn't hit out. That you've got to tell somebody.' Danny gives a snort of derision. 'What about Mr Court? You like him, don't you?'

'Yes, he's all right.'

'Then tell *him*.'

Danny shrugs. 'Maybe.'

But he won't. He won't tell anyone. He's new. He's got few friends, just Nikki and Tracey really. Nobody wants a grass around, especially when it's a new kid. No, if he wants this new life, if he wants his promised land, he's going to have to sort this out his own way.

'Danny, I want your word on this.'

'OK,' he says, 'You've got it.'

For what it's worth.

Des

He finishes his Chinese take-away and pushes the foil cartons aside. The TV is on low, a cable music channel. He isn't paying it much attention. From his window he can see the Edge. He wonders what Cathy and Danny are doing now. He tries to imagine their life with him in it. It's soft focus Walt Disney stuff. A man, his wife and his kid, usually walking along the beach kicking up the gentle waves. It's appealing. Then Des shakes his head. Too late, too damned late for him. He had his chance. Two chances in fact. Two women. Two children. He wasn't there for any of them.

He picks up his mobile and toys with the idea of phoning Cathy. Wouldn't old man Mangam flip if he knew Cathy had given him the number? After a few moments he puts the phone down again and closes his eyes.

No, too much water under the bridge.

Abbie

He is up in his room. He has just phoned Danny again. *Number unattainable.*

'For goodness' sake!' he groans, tossing the mobile on to his bed. 'Don't you ever have it switched on?'

Chris Kane's smile has been with him all evening. It was a smile of triumph.

'You know, don't you?' says Abbie. 'You know where Danny is.'

Which is more than Abbie does. Danny has never even said which county he's in. Abbie can understand it, of course. He'd be the same in Danny's place. But now Chris knows more than he does. Suddenly he is holding all the aces. Abbie sees the smile again, in his mind's eye, and shudders. No doubt about it. He's on the way, Danny, thinks Abbie. The psycho, The Animal, he's on his way.

'And I've no means of warning you.'

HARRY

He listens to the story of the interview with Mr King. He listens and he seethes. There is a lifetime of frustration and failure and missed opportunities in his growing anger. This is crazy. So this is modern education. What are they saying? You can't stand up for yourself any more! 'What's a lad supposed to do?' he asks. 'Just stand there and take it?'

He sees something in Cathy's face. Amusement maybe. Irritation, more like. He can guess what she's thinking. *You've changed your tune*. Well, maybe I have, Harry thinks. Maybe I'm beginning to look beyond the skin to the person inside. That's Danny's doing. It's taken a fifteen-year-old boy to make him see for the first time.

'Dad,' Cathy says finally. 'Can't we talk about this later?'

'Why?' asks Harry. 'What have you got to say to me that can't be said in front of Danny?'

Cathy squeezes her eyes in a pleading expression. 'No, I won't wait till later and I won't keep quiet. Tell me what Danny did wrong.'

Danny turns. The old man's rage matches his mood more than his mother's measured words. Danny looks interested in Cathy's answer.

'What do you want him to do?' Harry demands. 'Expect him to turn the other cheek, do you?'

'What I want Danny to do,' says Cathy, coolly, patiently. 'Is to try to follow the school rules. I've told Mr King I expect him to take action against these bullies, but he won't take much notice of me if Danny doesn't at least try it his way. I want him to report anything to the teachers.'

'And what will they do?' says Harry, an edge of scorn in his voice. 'Blame our Danny, that's what.'

Cathy sees Danny nodding and she feels anger rising. What right does he have to tell her how to bring up her son. Where's he been all these years? 'This is a bit rich coming from you, Dad. It's not long ago you didn't give either of us a moment's thought.'

The raised voices have drawn Joan into the living-room. Harry winces inside. Cathy will always be able to pull this little rabbit out of the hat, the fact that he turned his back on them all those years ago.

'Cathy,' he says. 'Don't you think I would turn the clock back if I could?' He glances at Danny and owns up to the wrong he has done. 'I'm sorry lad, I'm so sorry.' Then the softness falls from his voice. 'But that doesn't mean I'm not right now, Cathy.'

He looks at her from under his brows. 'There's only one thing the likes of Parker understand. It isn't teachers and fancy words. It isn't social workers and softly softly. He's too far gone for any of that to touch him.'

He balls his fist.

'It's this.'

Danny

By the time the old man has finished, his heart is thumping. He's right. Of course he's right. There's only one thing Steve Parker will understand, and that's when somebody comes along who is tougher than he is, harder than he is, more determined than he is. Danny almost laughs out loud. What a turn up for the book. Who'd have thought it?

Me siding with old Grumbleguts!

His grandfather's certainty, his call to arms sound so much more appealing that his mother's patient, gentle plea to give the school's way a try. Danny has had to take too much. He has had to swallow it all down, the filthy language, the sour looks, the abuse. He wants to hit back. He so wants to take the maggot that's twisting and turning in the heart of the Edge and crush it into slime.

Mum catches up with him. 'Danny, you won't do anything stupid, will you?'

'No Mum, I won't do anything stupid.'

Mum's face relaxes, but only until Danny speaks again.

'But I will do something.' He walks into his room. As he closes the door he hears her voice:

'Danny . . .'

He signals the end of their conversation. 'Goodnight Mum.'

Cathy

She stands looking at the closed door. For a moment she thinks about walking in and having it out with him. But she has seen the hooded look.

She doesn't know what is going on in Danny's head, but she knows that anything she says to him now is bound to backfire. You don't understand, Danny. I'm not going to let you down. If the school doesn't sort this out, I'll be the first to go round and see those young thugs. But you don't want to listen to what I've got to say right now, I understand that. It's better to walk away.

'Goodnight, Danny love.'

She sees the lights of the Edge pulsing like distant stars. She sees the headlights of a car on the moors road, making its way down from the motorway. What she doesn't know is that the car is a black Ford Mondeo – and that it is being driven by Chris Kane.

15

Chris

So where do you start, Chrissie old son?

He has been looking out over the town from his vantage point up on the moors road, basking in the promise of that blanket of lights. The Mangams are ex-directory, he knows that already. No joy from the phone book then, but that's just a minor inconvenience. He is no more than a heartbeat away from her now. It is like watching the ripples from a stone tossed into a pond, but in reverse, each circle tightening round his prey. He can almost smell her hair, touch her skin, taste the salty tang of her tears. He checks the time. Getting late. There's nothing to be done tonight. He drives down the long, winding gradient that leads into the town then cruises the darkened streets for a while, smiling as he looks at the terraced houses. She could be in any one of them. Who knows? He could be looking at her lighted window right now.

Do you know I'm here, Cathy girl? Can you sense the big bad wolf? A-woooo.

He imagines standing in the doorway, the avenging angel, the man reclaiming his woman, his manhood. In his mind's eye he is swatting aside the brat, Danny her puny defender. Instinctively he rubs at his cheek, recalling the affront at the tube station. Finally, he grows bored of the game, imagining her at her fireside, so cosy, so unsuspecting. He sees a sign for the railway station and hangs a left. Where there are stations

140

there are hotels. He pulls up outside the Royal, just up the road from the station. It's nothing to write home about, not much more than a glorified pub really, with a few upstairs rooms. But it will do.

'Can I help you, sir?' asks a tall, blonde woman as he walks in.

Chris glances over the counter. Nice legs, he notes. Not a patch on his Cathy's though. The name tag identifies her as Margaret.

'I'd like a room,' he says. 'Margaret.'

She gives a neutral smile. She's obviously used to customers flirting. Don't worry Margaret, he thinks, I've no designs on you. A one-woman man, that's Chrissie Kane. Margaret runs through the usual spiel: prices, wake-up calls, breakfast times.

'Anything else?' she asks. 'Newspaper perhaps?'

He shakes his head. There's only one world he is interested in, the world according to Chris Kane. What use does he have for Today in Parliament, news round-ups or *and finallys*? They make no difference to him. He turns and heads for the stairs. He has just set a foot on the first step when something occurs to him.

'There is one thing,' he says. 'Do you know how many secondary schools there are round here?'

'Secondary schools?'

'Yes, my . . . my nephew is at a local school. I wanted to surprise him. I'm trying to remember the name.'

Margaret pulls out a phone book and finds a list of schools. 'I could photocopy the page if you like,' she says.

'That would be really helpful.'

She disappears into a small office. He sees the flash of the photocopier. 'There you go, sir,' she says, offering him a folded sheet of A4 paper. Chris holds out a 20p coin in return. 'That's all right,' she says. 'A single copy is neither here nor there. I hope you enjoy your stay.'

Chris thinks of Cathy, not a heartbeat away. 'Don't worry,' he says, 'I will.'

Danny

It is the next morning. It is blustery over the Edge. Danny meets Nikki at the walkway where the cold is piercing and raw. Tracey peels away from them and catches up with a group of girls walking about twenty yards ahead.

'What did Kingy say to you?' asks Nikki.

'Nothing worth listening to.' Nikki gives a sympathetic smile. 'All he could see was a black kid with a chip on his shoulder. He talked to me as if it was my fault.'

'He would,' says Nikki. 'All he's bothered about is appearances. No trouble, that's the main thing. Keep it all under wraps. He wants to keep the parents from Hazel Bank happy.'

'From where?'

'Hazel Bank. It's a couple of miles up the road. Detached houses. Range Rovers. Kingy will do anything to suck up to them.'

'Including throwing me to the wolves?'

'Of course.'

They walk towards the school gates, huddled together against the biting wind. They see Steve from a distance. 'Maybe we should hang around here for a few minutes,' Nikki suggests. 'Give him time to go in.'

'I'm not backing off,' says Danny, straightening his back and taking the sting of the wind on his thin, proud face. 'Not on account of that muppet.' Nikki gives him a sideways look. 'What?' Danny asks.

'I think you're very brave,' says Nikki. She doesn't mean it as a compliment, because she immediately adds: 'Maybe a bit too brave for your own good. You know what they say about people who stick their head above the parapet?'

Danny raises an eyebrow, waiting for the punchline.

'They get it shot off.'

Danny snakes his arm round her, feeling the muscle round

her waist and the bottom of her rib cage and he gives her a playful squeeze.

'Thanks for caring.'

Chris

Chris has crossed the Catholic school off his list. Hardly likely. He and Cathy never discussed religion much but he is pretty sure she's C of E, at least by upbringing. Besides, if he draws a blank at the two remaining schools he can always come back to St Teresa's. He parks the black Mondeo in a cul-de-sac and saunters up the road. He buys a paper from a newsagent's and leans against a wall. He has the paper open at the TV section but keeps his eyes on the school gates. Once or twice his heart skips a beat as he thinks he sees Danny. On closer inspection he discovers it isn't him. Soon the stream of kids has slowed to a trickle.

'Excuse me,' he asks a group of stragglers, 'There isn't a back gate or anything, is there?'

They shake their heads.

That's it then. It's got to be Edgecliff High.

See you tonight, Danny boy.

Danny

He approaches the gates without breaking his stride. He can feel Nikki dragging on him. Sorry, he thinks, but Danny Mangam doesn't back down, not to a bag of puke like Steve Parker.

'Look what the cat's dragged in,' says Craig, tugging at Steve's sleeve.

'You've got a nerve coming back here,' says Steve. His nose is taped. The swelling is obvious under the ridiculous dressing.

'Broken?' asks Danny.

'What do you think?'

'Good,' says Danny. 'Reminds me of a joke. How does Steve Parker smell with a broken nose? Terrible.'

Danny can hear the intake of breath from Nikki. He doesn't care. This is one junior Ku Kluxer who won't forget his name in a hurry. Danny Mangam's made his mark.

'Think you're a funny guy, don't you?' says Steve.

'I know you are,' Danny shoots back. 'What with the red nose and all. When do you get the long shoes and the revolving bow tie?'

Steve's eyes narrow. 'I'm going to wipe that smile off your face, chocolate drop,' he says.

Danny shrugs and pushes between Steve and Craig. Craig grabs his sleeve. Danny stops and glares at the offending hand. 'You've got ten seconds to get your mitts off me.'

'Stop it, you two,' says Nikki. 'Kingy's watching. Look, at the window.'

Craig lets go and Danny walks on into school.

'You don't need to do that,' Nikki hisses. 'You're asking for trouble.'

'Maybe I am,' says Danny. 'What's new? I've had trouble all my life.'

In a flash of memory he sees Mum kneeling on the floor trying to get up and Chris standing over her like a victorious boxer. But that's not all. He sees himself, or at least the boy he was, standing in a corner, just looking on. For three years shame has been an infection inside him, sour and spreading.

I just stood and watched while he beat on her.

There is only one way to make the shame go away and that is to never stand by or back off or walk away ever again.

'What do you mean?' asks Nikki. 'What trouble?' Danny looks away. 'Danny, what trouble?'

He watches Steve and Craig walking down the corridor. 'Forget it.'

'But Danny . . .'

'I said forget it.'

144

Chris

With a few hours to kill, he wanders into the town centre. He sits smoking on the wall round an ornamental flower-bed, watching the girls go by. Actually, girls are few and far between at this time of the day. It's mostly pensioners, with the odd young mother pushing a buggy towards the Post Office to collect her child benefit. Chris isn't good at killing time. He doesn't read and he doesn't enjoy his own company. Too many uncomfortable thoughts, too many demons. He glances at his watch, willing the hours to go by. It turns out he has been sitting on the wall for less than ten minutes.

With a sigh he sets off towards the run-down, Sixties-built shopping arcade.

He hovers outside a café, one of those small affairs attached to a baker's, then decides to try room service back at the hotel.

Cathy

She is thinking about Des, and not in the vague, distracted way she has thought about him over the years. Seeing him face to face has brought it all back. She has had three relationships since Des, but none of them has come close to what she had with him. Now it's all there, the butterflies, the racing pulse, the prickling that flows over her skin. She rubs at the table she is cleaning, rubs so hard she attracts one customer's attention.

'You'll take the surface off,' says old George from his usual seat at the back.

Cathy smiles. 'I was miles away,' she says.

'Thinking about some lad, were you?'

'Hardly a lad,' says Cathy.

She moves to the next table, piling the cups and plates on a tray. She is making her way to the counter with the tray when she sees . . .

No, it can't be!

She sees *him*.

The tray falls from her hands. Cups and plates break, cold coffee spills on the tiled floor.

'Something wrong?' asks George anxiously. Cathy doesn't answer. Instead she flies to the door and looks down Edgecliff Walk. There is no sign of him. 'Are you all right?'

She focuses on George's kindly, concerned face.

'Yes, yes I'm fine. I thought . . .' She starts to clear up the mess. 'It's all right, I'm imagining things.'

Imagining Chris Kane. But he isn't here. He couldn't be.

Danny

'Think you're the big man, don't you?' sneers Steve.

He's just intercepted Danny outside the canteen. Mr King has been trying to get the kids to call it the refectory, but canteen has stuck. Craig and Jamie are in tow. They join in. The jibes are like water off a duck's back, until Steve speaks again.

'Something you should know about Nikki,' he says. 'She's a bit of a bike.'

He winks. 'Been round a bit, if you know what I mean. I've been there myself.'

Danny knows what Steve's trying to do – spoil something that's been making the Edge tolerable. He manages to keep the lid on his anger.

'She's told me about you and her,' he says. 'Two dates, and you didn't even get a kiss.'

His words get a reaction. He knows from the look on Steve's face that Nikki has told him the truth. He sees Craig and Jamie turn towards Steve. He's obviously told them differently.

'Doesn't mean she isn't a slapper,' says Steve.

'No?' Danny retorts. 'But she turned you down. So what does that say about you, Parker?'

Steve glances at his mates. He's squirming visibly. 'I think it's time you put your money where your mouth is, chocolate drop,' he snarls. 'Me and you after school. Pick your venue.'

'Don't you think you ought to let the nose heal first?' says Danny.

'What for? I could take you with two broken arms.'

'You know what?' says Danny, turning away. 'You're pathetic.'

'That's it, run away.'

Danny feels a heat rash starting at the nape of his neck and working down his spine. He grits his teeth and keeps on walking.

'I'll see you later, Mangam,' Steve calls after him.

Danny reaches the end of the corridor. As he turns left to reach the computer suite he shoots back a defiant:

'Not if I see you first.'

Cathy

She is sitting outside with Debbie, the other waitress at the café. It's quiet and the manager is holding the fort. They have brought a packet of sandwiches each, a cake and a Coke.

'You're quiet,' says Debbie.

'I thought I saw somebody,' says Cathy. 'A face from the past.'

'Ex-boyfriend?'

Cathy picks at a loose thread on her uniform. 'Something like that.'

'But it wasn't him?'

Cathy shakes her head. 'Couldn't have been. I did a runner. No forwarding address.'

'Why, did he knock you about?' Cathy stares straight ahead. 'He did, didn't he?'

Cathy nods her head.

'I went out with a lad like that,' says Debbie. 'Real psycho. He'd slap me around then burst into tears. They're like that, macho man one minute, little boy lost the next.'

Cathy looks at Debbie. Psycho. Did you hear that, Cathy girl. The psycho. What if it was him? You can't just sit here. Do something, for goodness' sake. She stands up abruptly.

'I've got to make a phone call,' she says. She hurries back inside and dials home. When Mum answers she puts her money in. 'Mum? Hi, it's me. Has anybody called today?'

Mum asks who she's expecting.

'Oh nobody.' She realises how stupid that must sound. 'It's OK, Mum. I thought . . .'

She doesn't know what to say next. Oh, don't be stupid. It couldn't be him. It just couldn't.

'It's all right. Just forget it.'

Cathy puts the phone down. Her heart is beating fast. Forget it. That's easier said than done.

Joan

Joan can't forget it either. At first she thinks Cathy might be talking about Des, but there is no disguising the shake in her voice. No, it isn't Des. Joan knows her daughter. She's scared, terrified even. Joan stands looking at the phone, as if willing it to give up its secrets. It's him, isn't it, the psycho she's talked about. Does this mean he's coming? Is he already here? Maybe Harry will be needing his baseball bat after all.

Chris

Same routine as this morning. Pull up in a side street. Stroll on down to the school gates. This time he is armed with the evening paper. He glances at his watch. Five past three. He wonders how long they'll be. Could be ten past. Could be half past. Sometimes schools are even later.

'Come on, Danny boy,' he says. 'Let's be having you.' He looks at the school sign. Edgecliff High School. Headmaster: R King. 'I wonder if you're anything like fatboy Dickson.'

Not that it will make much difference.

He doesn't plan to confront Danny here. No, this time he's going to use his head and follow the brat home. No sense spooking him before he's led the way to Cathy. By twenty past the streets are still quiet so Chris walks into a newsagents and buys a can of Fanta. As he drinks the ice-cold liquid he thinks of Cathy.

Where are you? What's the closest I've come to you?

He smiles, thinking of the look on her face when he arrives on the doorstep. Little pink pig faces big bad wolf. And there'll be no keeping him out of that brick house.

Des

What the hell, he thinks, I'm going to do it. I'm going to phone them.

His marriage was a mistake, but not Cathy. No, that was the real thing, as much as any relationship is the real thing. To think he let her go just to patch up his marriage. Like that was going to work! By the time he realised what he was giving up, she'd gone, left the Edge. And it was for good, as far as he knew. No forwarding address, nothing.

Not that old man Mangam would have given it to him if he had it.

He looks at his watch and wonders what time she gets home. He decides to phone the café first. At least that way old man Mangam isn't going to pick up the phone.

Danny

Danny is waiting for Nikki outside the language lab. She has French last lesson. For want of anything else to do he starts pulling things out of his blazer pocket. He produces his mobile. He wonders why he bothers to bring it at all. You have to keep it switched off in school. Come to think of it, he's hardly had it switched on since he got here. He feels a pang of guilt. Abbie, Ramila, he hasn't given them a moment's thought in days. Some friend he is.

He switches the mobile on. He could even give Abbie a call now. School will be out. He glances at the screen. Ten text messages. Danny smiles. Abbie's been busy. But as he scrolls through the messages his eyes grow hard, his face tightens. The messages fill him with horror:

He's coming.

Danny, he's on his way.

He knows where you are.

He's after you. The Animal's after you.

'No, *no!*'

He reads each one of the increasingly desperate messages. They all say the same thing. He's coming. Chris is coming.

Chris

About time!

Kids are streaming through the gates laughing, joking, play-fighting. He watches them keenly, trying to spot one face in the crowd.

Let's be having you, Danny boy. The big bad wolf wants his dinner.

He watches and he watches. Finally he is rewarded. There, walking through the gates with a cute little blonde, is Danny boy. Well well, thinks Chris, we are growing up. Big enough to pull the birds, big enough to smack your uncle Chrissie in the kisser. But big enough to keep the wolf from the door?

I don't think so somehow.

Danny

'You're scaring me,' says Nikki. 'I've never seen you like this. Please Danny, talk to me. Is it something I've done?'

Danny stares at her as if she's speaking a foreign language. 'Something you've done? Of course not.' They are walking across the patch of waste ground that used to be a factory.

'What then? What's wrong?' He shows her his text messages. 'The Animal? Who's this animal?'

'His name's Chris. Mum used to live with him.'

'But why does that matter?'

Danny tells her. He spares her the worst details, giving only the briefest outline of events. Even that is enough to make her eyes go wide with fright.

'And he's coming after your mum?'

'I think so. I've got to phone Abbie, find out what he knows.'

But before he can punch in the number, the mobile is slapped from his hand. 'What the . . . ?'

'Well, if it isn't the chocolate drop.'

Danny looks straight into the eyes of Steve Parker. 'Give me that phone.'

Steve picks it up. 'What, this?'

'Danny holds out his hand. 'Stop messing and give me the phone.'

He takes a step forward but Steve chucks the mobile to Craig. Craig passes it to Jamie and he tosses it to Keith. So he's resurfaced. Keith returns it to Steve. Steve gives a cold smile.

'Still want it?'

Danny reaches for the mobile. Steve waits until he almost has it then smashes it down on the block of concrete. 'Oops, clumsy me.'

Danny rugby-tackles Steve, throwing him to the ground. He is about to land a punch when Craig catches him with a right hand that makes his senses blur. Everything seems cloudy, distant. Through the haze he hears Nikki.

'Leave him alone! Please, don't hurt him.'

That's when he realises that he is on the ground, being kicked and punched. The toe of a shoe catches him in the face. A fist slams into his ribs. Then another kick thuds into his back, sending the pain whipcracking up his spine. He tastes blood, salty and thick in his mouth. He's getting the worst of it.

Steve, Keith and Craig are on top of him, maybe Jamie as well. He reaches out an arm, desperate to raise himself to his feet. At least standing, he will have a fighting chance.

Before he can scramble even to his knees a heel stamps down on his hand, sending the pain crackling up his arm. He hears a scream and recognises it as his own. The pain in his wounded hand is fiery and sharp. It hurts like hell, not least because it brings to mind Mum's broken hand. Danny is like her now, reduced to a victim, pummelled, beaten, made less than human.

That's when another thought goes through his mind. Nikki, what are they doing to Nikki? He manages to hoist himself up on to all fours. He looks up. It's Keith, Craig and Jamie who are on top of him now. Nikki is struggling with Steve.

'Leave her alone!' Danny yells.

'Come on, Nikki, give me a kiss. You've not been too choosy just lately.'

'Leave her alone!'

The words come out strangely. Danny realises that his lips and cheeks are already swelling. He is trying to get to his feet when he sees a foot swinging right at his head. The impact propels him backwards, leaving him flat on his back, winded and defenceless. He braces himself for the worst.

Des

'Hi,' he says, 'Is Cathy Mangam there?'

It's somebody called Debbie. She tells him that Cathy's gone. Trouble at home.

'Did she say what sort?'

The voice at the other end of the line is guarded, suspicious. This Debbie girl obviously thinks she's said too much already. 'No, just that she had to go.'

Des puts the phone down. Trouble? He remembers the boys that had circled Danny like a pack of wolves stalking a deer. His chest feels tight and his heartbeat is raised.

The price of caring.

Cathy

'You're early,' says Mum the moment Cathy walks into the house.

Cathy looks around. Her eyes are haunted.

'Cathy, what's wrong?'

Cathy does her best to look composed. 'Nothing.'

'Don't give me that. I'm not stupid. It's him, isn't it?'

Cathy sits down in an armchair then immediately stands again.

'It is, isn't it?' says Mum. 'It's this Chris.'

Cathy turns and faces her mother. She nods. 'Mum, he's evil.'

'But you said he didn't know where you were.'

'That newspaper you sent me,' says Cathy. 'It's still in the flat.'

Joan stares, trying to remember the newspaper. Cathy explains her suspicions.

'Are you sure it was him you saw?' asks Mum.

Cathy shakes her head. 'No, not sure. But Mum, what if it was, what if he finds us?'

Danny

He curls his knees up to his stomach and throws up his arms protectively. The blow never comes. For a moment he thinks he knows the rescuer's identity. It's Des again, making a habit of saving his bacon.

But when Danny looks up he finds himself staring into the face of Chris Kane.

'Having a spot of bother, Danny boy?'

Steve comes into view. 'Look mate,' he says, 'I don't know what your problem is, but why don't you just push off?'

Chris grins. It's a smile Danny's seen a hundred times before, the prelude to terror.

'Go on,' says Steve, 'Clear off or else.'

Chris folds his arms across his chest, the leather jacket making a creaking noise. 'Or else what exactly?'

For a moment Danny is about to warn Steve. Then the urge goes. If a fight breaks out it might just give him time to get away. Steve, Jamie and Craig take a step forward. Keith starts to drift away from the action.

'Don't be silly,' says Chris, uncrossing his arms.

'Look , what's this got to do with you anyway?'

Steve doesn't finish the sentence. Chris unleashes a vicious uppercut. There's a sickening blow. Danny knows that his tormentor now has a broken jaw to add to the nose. Craig is the next to fall victim to The Animal, taking a kick in the solar plexus. He drops to his knees, retching violently.

'Nikki run!' cries Danny, taking off towards the Edge. 'Find a phone and call my house. Tell them what's happened.'

Nikki starts running. Danny can feel Chris behind him. Even though every step sends a jarring pain through his body he isn't going to stop. Not until he's warned Mum.

Cathy

She takes Nikki's call.

'Oh God no!'

'What is it?' asks Mum.

'It's him. He turned up at the school.'

'Has he got Danny?'

Cathy's face is ashen. She seems unable to speak. The truth is, her mind is reeling. She can't even think.

'Who is this?' asks Joan, taking the phone from Cathy. 'Nikki? Listen love, take it slowly and tell me everything. Has this man got Danny? No. You're sure? That's something at least. No, you leave this to us.'

She hangs up. 'Cathy, I'll phone the police. You go and tell your Dad. He's pointing that back wall.'

Cathy stares at her mother, seemingly unable to comprehend.

'Do it.'

Cathy nods and goes to him. For the first time since she was a little girl, she is asking for his help.

16

Danny

He is struggling up the Edge, holding his ribs. Gone is his usual
easy running style. His breathing is laboured and painful. Steve
and his mates have done some serious damage. His legs are
leaden, but he is still outpacing Chris. It doesn't occur to him
that Chris might be letting him stay in front, leading him to
Cathy. He's too scared to think straight. Danny glances round.
There goes The Animal running back to his car. For a moment
Danny wonders why Chris doesn't follow on foot, then he
hears the tyres screech and a plume of black smoke rise. Chris
accelerates towards the hill road. He stops thinking and runs.
As Danny forces his bruised body the last few strides to the top
of the Edge he finds the words of that ridiculous chant going
through his mind the way it did on the cross-country.

With-out fear.

With-out fear.

Danny Mangam's without fear.

But he isn't and maybe he never will be. The Animal is back,
and with him the nightmare of terror without end. He is here
in the promised land and he is going to make a mockery of the
freedom Mum and Danny thought they had won. Danny sees
the black Mondeo coming up the hill road and drives on, his
feet pounding on the thin turf, sending shockwaves through
his body. Not the café, no, I can't go there. I'd be leading him
right to Mum. Maybe I can lose him on the Edge. I've found

156

loads of short cuts while I've been running. Yes, then I can make it home unseen. I can phone Mum from there, tell her to steer clear of the house. That way I'll keep him away from her, at least for now. Until we can think of something, get help from somebody. Danny can hear the roar of the car's engine. But he won't give up. He's got to keep on going. He's got to warn Mum.

Chris

He knows he has to get this just right. He owes a debt to those boys who were giving Danny boy a pasting. They've really rattled the brat. Danny isn't thinking straight or he wouldn't be running like this, leading the big bad wolf to the piggies' little brick house. Chris eases through the gear box. But you're thinking straight, Mr Big Bad Wolf. Follow in the car, so you can throw the lovely Cathy in the back and speed off before anybody notices.

Chris concentrates. He has got to drive fast enough to convince Danny boy that this is a real chase, but not so fast that he actually catches the boy.

What he wants is for Danny to lead him to the house, to Cathy.

Chris is smiling in anticipation of the sensations he is about to savour: the sight of Cathy's face, those lovely eyes wide in terror; the sound of her pleading with him not to touch her; finally the feel of a roll of crisp twenty-pound notes. His woman, his cash. His manhood restored.

HARRY

'What are you doing?' asks Cathy.

'Phoning Danny's mobile.'

'There's no point. Nikki saw those lads smash it. She told me.'

'Maybe I should drive up there,' says Harry.

Cathy looks at him. She seems to be turning the idea over in her mind. 'No,' she says finally. 'It isn't Danny he wants. It's me. With or without Danny, he'll be coming here.'

Harry nods. It makes some sort of sense. If there *is* any sense in this crazy world. So this is why she came home. To flee from a madman. Cathy hasn't had a lot of time for explanations, but she's said enough.

'I'll be ready for him then,' says Harry.

Suddenly Joan is right there in front of him, barring his way. Now, with this lunatic heading for them, the baseball bat doesn't seem such a good idea. 'What are you going to do?'

Harry knows exactly what he is going to do. He's going to put things right. He is going to be a father to his daughter, a grandfather to his grandson. He's going to do what he should have done fifteen years ago. He is going to take sides, to stand up for Cathy and Danny.

'I'm going to defend my family.'

'Harry, don't do anything silly,' says Joan pleadingly. 'This is a strong young man. We've got to try to reason with him, delay him until the police get here.'

'You delay him, Joan, but if he tries to set a foot in this house I'll be here to stop him, any way I can.'

Without another word he walks upstairs and kneels down by the bed. He reaches for the baseball bat.

Danny

He sees the war memorial up ahead. It's my war now, he thinks, Danny's war against fear. He pounds past the memorial and plunges down the slope to a path further down the Edge. Chris won't be able to follow here, at least not in the car. Steadying himself on reaching the path, Danny starts to run in the direction of Cork Terrace. He can't believe that The Animal is here. How could it happen? Mum said she didn't leave a trace. So how? How?

He glances back up the slope. He can't see Chris from here, or the road for that matter. He can hear the car though. Danny wonders for a moment if he is doing the right thing. But what else can he do? There's just one idea in his head. Home, got to get home and phone Mum from there. If he can lose Chris along the way, great; but sometime, somehow, they will have to face him. He isn't going to go away.

Almost there.

He races down the slope, recklessly, madly, pain ratcheting through him. Just that one thought in his mind. Get out of sight and make it home. Warn Mum.

He hopes against hope that he can't be seen from the top road, that he has given Chris the slip. But no such luck. There he is. The black Mondeo has just turned into the estate.

He's seen me!

Danny pushes himself on, turning into Cork Terrace just ahead of the Mondeo. He sees the front door open. There's Grandad waving him in. Thank God for old Grumbleguts! But that's the last of the good news. The moment he slams the door behind him he sees her.

'Mum! What are you doing here?'

'Danny, your face!'

'Forget my face. I'll live. Why are you here? You should have stayed at work. Why didn't you stay away? He's back. The Animal's back.' As if to hammer home the point a knock comes on the door. 'It's him.'

159

It's as though the world is spinning round Danny, seen from a carousel. Mum, white-faced and staring, Gran shaking visibly, Grandad holding, of all things, a baseball bat. It's all like a crazy dream. Then it gets even crazier. Chris's voice comes through the letter box.

'Don't shut me out, Cathy. Open the door now. We've got to talk.'

After everything he's done. He wants to *talk*!

'I love you, Cathy. There's no need for all this. I love you.'

PC Daniels

Neither PC Kate Daniels nor PC Dave Lancashire can make head nor tail of the two calls. The first sends them to number three, Cork Terrace, to tell Steve Parker's parents that he has been the victim of a serious assault and is in the General. The second comes a few minutes later, and takes precedence. It tells them to go next door to number one, Cork Terrace. Another assault, also involving a teenage boy and an unknown adult male. Possible trouble at the house itself.

'Coincidence?' asks PC Daniels, thinking out loud.

PC Lancashire shakes his head slowly. 'I can't see it. So young Parker's got his come-uppance. Couldn't happen to a nicer lad.'

They accelerate up the Edgecliff road, intrigued by the two calls. PC Daniels remembers the last time she saw Steve Parker and tries to put the pieces together. She comes up with . . . nothing.

Chris

That's the moment it all comes together. Love and terror, needing and owning. She's there, at the other side of the door. His Cathy, with his money. He's going to teach her a lesson. First he will teach her to cross him, then he will teach her to love him. His Cathy living according to his rules.

'Go away, Chris,' she shouts from the other side of the door. 'Go back to London. It's over.'

'No,' he yells back. 'It isn't over. It won't be over until I tell you so.'

He slams his fist into the door, crashes against it with his shoulder. All reason is gone now. What is his is waiting on the other side of that door, and he will have it any way he can. 'Cathy, don't make this difficult. Come out and talk.' But even as he is asking her to talk he is booting the door, feeling the resistance of a seven-lever mortice. Harry's handiwork.

He hears her voice again, pleading, frightened: 'Please Chris, just leave us alone.'

Leave them alone! Him, Chrissie Kane, the man who has fed them and loved them and given them everything. Him, leave them alone?

'Never.'

With a shout of fury he boots the door again.

Danny

'Maybe we should run for it,' he says.

Mum manages a smile, in spite of everything, then touches his arm. 'The condition you're in?' she says. 'I don't know how you got this far. No, the safest bet is to sit tight. And if he gets

161

in . . .' She glances at Harry. 'We'll do what we have to. I'm not going back.'

'Where are the police?' says Joan, trembling with fright. 'Why are they taking so long?'

Harry is standing, still as a statue, not speaking, just clinging to the baseball bat.

Danny hears the crash of The Animal as he pounds the door, hurling himself against it in his desperate attempt to beat it down.

'Will it hold?' Danny asks Grandad. 'Will it keep him out?'

Grandad gives a little jerk of the head, neither nod nor shake, simply a gesture of acknowledgement. It is a question to which he doesn't have the answer.

'Go away!' yells Danny, marching up the hall. 'Leave us alone! Why can't you just leave us alone!'

Des

'I'll be back in an hour,' he tells his two mechanics. 'If anyone calls, take their number.'

He picks up his car keys and walks through the concertina doors to where his car is parked. He's afraid, him a grown man, afraid of what Cathy and Danny might say. He is afraid of their anger, their disappointment, their recriminations. But there is no putting it off. He has to face his past, start to put things right. Maybe, just maybe, it isn't too late to have a family. If I could only turn back time, he thinks. If I could meet myself as a young man. The things I'd tell him!

He climbs into the driver's seat and starts the car. Then a thought occurs to him. Trouble, that girl said there was trouble. It'll be old man Mangam, I bet. But for him, we might just have made it. With that thought in his head, that they could have made it, that they might make it yet, he pulls away from the pavement and drives off down the road.

Chris

So, the little piggies won't come out. Fine, time for the big bad wolf to get serious. He looks around, noticing for the first time that he has an audience, a couple of pensioners, a few young mothers with toddlers, nothing to concern him. Then he sees the wheelie bin. It must have been emptied just this morning, so there it is, an open invitation. Chris picks it up and hurls it through the front window, sending a snowstorm of splintered glass spiralling into the house. Pulling out a couple of the bigger shards of glass he climbs through the shattered window pane.

'Cathy,' he roars. *'Ca-thee!'*

He plunges into the hallway. She's there, holding a chair. 'Don't be like that, Cath,' he says. 'I only want to talk.'

He takes a step forward and makes a grab for the chair Cathy is holding up to defend herself. As he does, he receives a glancing blow to the head that makes his senses swim. Through a mist of shock and surprise he sees Harry Mangam bracing himself for a second swing.

Want to play with the big boys, do you, old man?

Chris feels around and puts his hand on a wooden newspaper rack. It splinters under the impact of the baseball bat, but it has taken enough of the power out of the blow. Reacting quicker than the old man, he grabs the end of the bat, putting all his force into wrestling it from him. They grapple for a few moments, but it is an unequal contest. With a triumphant grin, Chris takes the bat.

'Dad!' cries Cathy.

'Run!' yells Harry. 'Get Joan and Danny out of here.'

Chris looks at the old man with hatred. It is his turn to swing.

HARRY

As he fights to hang on to the bat he finds himself cursing the years. He curses the lost years when he drove his family away. He curses all that wasted time that has seen his strength fade until he can't defend them.

'Get out of my house!' he yells, while at the same time waving Cathy away.

'Get out! Get out!' he roars at the psycho.

'Run!' he pleads to Cathy.

Then he loses his grip. He sees the bat swing and come flashing towards him. There is no time to think another thought before the blow thunders in his brain and everything goes black.

Cathy

'Harry!' screams Joan.

'*Ca-thee!*' The voice is hardly human, a primal, animal screech. A moment later Cathy appears.

'We've got to get out,' she pants. 'We've got to get help. Dad's down.' There is a heavy tread behind her. 'He's coming.'

Cathy rattles at the rusted bolt on the back gate and succeeds in wrenching it open. 'There's nothing we can do for Dad,' she cries, shoving Mum and Danny ahead of her. 'We've got to run. If we can get the police, the ambulance . . .'

She forces Mum out and persuades her to start running across the waste ground that leads to the Edge. Then she realises. Danny isn't with them. She turns and sees him going back into the yard.

'Danny, no!'

Des

There is a small crowd outside number one, Cork Terrace. He brakes abruptly, slewing the car across the road, and jumps out.

'What's going on?' he asks.

'Some lunatic,' he is informed. 'Threw a wheelie bin right through the window. We've heard screams.'

Des climbs through the window and discovers Harry Mangam lying groaning on the parlour floor. He opens the front door and shouts to the onlookers. 'Phone an ambulance. Quick.'

He sees the bemused faces. 'For goodness' sake, don't just stand there. Do something.'

Mrs Wilson from number seven goes to call 999. Mrs McCann from number twelve used to be a nurse. She goes in to Mr Mangam to do what she can. Satisfied that old man Mangam is being taken care of, Des rushes through the house looking for some sign of Danny or Cathy. He sees somebody at the back door. Tall, blond, armed with a baseball bat. Over the man's shoulder he can see Danny.

'What's going on here?' he demands.

The man turns.

'I'm taking back what's mine,' he says in reply.

Des knows immediately there is something wrong with this man. He has the glazed expression of a fighter eight rounds into a bout. All reason has gone, replaced by a stubborn, brutal determination to survive, to win at all costs.

'Listen,' Des says quietly. 'Put down the baseball bat. We can talk about this.'

But the blond man doesn't want to talk. Without warning he swings the bat, smashing a picture on the wall. He swings again, gouging out a huge lump of plaster. Des tries to duck under the bat and get to grips with the man. He takes a glancing blow on the shoulder, but succeeds in getting his arms round his assailant's waist.

Danny

He is still holding the small shovel he picked up to use against Chris. He stares at Des grappling with The Animal. What's Des doing here? How did he know? But the important thing is, he's here. They have a chance. He sees Chris throw Des back against the wall and punch him hard in the chest. Des throws his arms round Chris, managing to cushion the next blow and half-climb over Chris's back. But Chris is strong.

He has the insane strength of a wounded, cornered creature. He lifts Des right off his feet and slams him into the door frame. Des wheezes but comes back again, clinging to the younger man.

I've got to do something.

'Des,' yells Danny. 'Let go.'

The moment Des steps aside Danny strikes out with the shovel. He makes contact but Chris just seems to shrug off the blow. Danny sees him looming in the doorway. He throws a punch, but Chris swats it aside.

'Think you can take me, do you?' pants The Animal. 'Well, think again. You might just be getting too big for your boots.'

Des tries to come back at Chris, but Chris elbows him in the stomach, winding him. Chris comes on, stepping into the yard. Danny retreats to the open gate. Chris is almost on top of him. Bracing himself, Danny throws a punch. This time he has more luck, his fist thudding into Chris's cheek. It gives Des time to recover. He runs forward, twisting Chris's arm up his back and forcing him face-first against the wall. Danny feels a surge of hope.

We've got him.

PC Kate Daniels

She is the first through the door. She sees a woman bending over a man in his late fifties or early sixties. She is trying to make him comfortable.

'He's through there,' says the woman.

PC Dave Lancashire overtakes her in the hallway. The scene in the house is chaos: broken glass, bits of plaster, flecks of blood. When they reach the yard they see two men. One of them has the other up against the wall. She recognises the aggressor. The Dark Angel.

'OK, sir,' says PC Lancashire. 'Let him go.'

'No,' says the Dark Angel. 'You don't understand.'

'I said, let him go.'

'I can't.'

The two PCs grab the Dark Angel roughly by the arms and pull him off. He starts to struggle. They react by dragging him round and pushing him to the ground. At that very moment a teenage boy runs forward.

'Dad!' he cries.

The second man, tall, blond and powerful-looking, lunges at the boy.

'Dave!' screams PC Daniels, 'I think we've made a terrible mistake.'

Chris

He can't believe his luck. Stupid coppers. He was finished, completely overpowered, and they've given him his chance. He sees them lying on top of the black guy and drives his boot into the male copper's ribs. He tries to get some more kicks in, the last aimed at the black guy's head, but he only manages to stumble over the woman's threshing legs. That's when he sees Danny boy blocking the gateway.

'Out there, is she?' he pants. 'Get out of the way.'

'Never!' shouts Danny defiantly.

Chris smiles. What's that? *Not by the hair on your chinny, chin, chin?* We'll see about that, Danny boy. This is the big, bad wolf you're dealing with.

He launches himself at Danny, pushing the boy backwards on to the waste ground. Danny stumbles and falls. Chris laughs out loud at the sight of the brat lying flat on his back, feet pedalling and kicking in a pathetic attempt at self-defence.

Time to do what he should have done a long time ago. Time to put him in his place.

'No!'

Cathy's voice stops him in his tracks. At last. There she is, right in front of him. After all the searching, all the fighting and screaming, there she is.

His Cathy.

Danny

'Mum, no.'

He picks himself up and stands at her side. 'Why did you come back?'

'Danny, I had to. I can't spend my life asking other people to fight my battles for me.'

He looks across at Chris. After the explosion of violence he seems strangely quiet. He is just standing there, recovering his breath. 'Get your things, Cathy. Get into the car. We're going home.'

'No Chris, no we're not.'

He makes a grab for her. She takes a step back. There is a look of revulsion on her face.

'I'm not going anywhere with you. I don't care if you're stronger than me. Force me to go with you and I'll run away at the first stop. Drag me back to London and I'll escape at the first opportunity. I'll jump out of the window, take the hinges off the door, I'll even claw my way through the brickwork if I have to. Whatever it takes, I'll get away.'

Danny is ready to fight, to do anything to get Chris off her. But there is no need. He isn't moving at all. He seems confused.

'But why, Cathy? Why did you leave me?'

'It's simple Chris, I don't love you. You can't scare somebody into loving you.'

He stares at her, his blue eyes cold and penetrating. 'No, you're not walking away from me, Cathy. It isn't that easy.'

Danny sees Des and the two police officers at the gate. He gives a little shake of his head to tell them to wait.

'I didn't say it was easy, Chris. I just said I was going to do it. You see, it doesn't really matter what you do now. You can hit me, hurt me all you like, but you'll never have me. You can't make me want to be with you.'

'Is it him?' asks Chris, 'Is he what all this is about? The black guy?'

'No,' says Cathy. 'It isn't another man. I'm not with *anybody*. There's me and there's Danny. That's my life, Chris. You're not in it.'

Danny watches the emotions drifting across Chris's face like stormclouds across the moon. For a moment, he thinks he is going to turn and walk away. But only for a moment. Two more police officers have arrived. One has his hand on his truncheon. Another is fingering the pouch that contains a pepper spray canister. Chris glances round at them.

'No Chris,' says Cathy. 'Don't.'

Chris

But Chris is not going to give up. He already knows he has lost. But he is still going to fight. To come all this way and not to fight for your woman, that would be cowardice. Cathy has

169

robbed him of his money, his life. She won't rob him of his manhood. As long as he is standing, as long as he can fight, he is still a man. Head turned, he keeps his eyes trained on the four police and the black guy. Lousy odds, but what the heck, who says this is about winning? It's about keeping your rep.

'Just come quietly please, sir,' says the woman PC.

Chris smiles. Quietly. Name a time when Chrissie Kane has ever come quietly. He smiles.

'That's it,' she says. 'Easy does it. Don't you think there's been enough damage done today?'

Chris smiles again. *Enough* damage? The lines from a TV cop show flash through his mind: *Lady, you ain't seen nothing yet.*

He turns and looks directly at Cathy. Then, with an animal roar, he hurls himself at her.

Danny

The police are on him before he can reach Mum. Instinctively, Danny has stepped in front of her and he feels the squeeze of her hands on his upper arms. He turns and gives her a thin smile.

In front of him, the fight is in its last moments. What seemed so monstrous and terrible inside the little house has become almost comic here in the open air. Chris looks pathetic, wriggling against the arms that are pinning him, like one of those old films of Houdini fighting his way out of a straitjacket. But Chris isn't going to escape. A police van is bumping across the waste ground, siren whooping. Then the female PC snaps the handcuffs on Chris. He will still struggle, resisting all the attempts of the police to calm him, but he is finished. He might not go quietly, but he will go.

'Grandad!' cries Danny, running into the house. He sees the old man being stretchered towards an ambulance. 'Will he be all right?' Danny asks the paramedic.

'He's conscious,' she replies. 'That's a good sign. We'll have the doctors check him out.'

'But will he be all right?'

The paramedic hesitates.

'You've got to tell me something,' says Danny.

The paramedic gives the briefest of nods. Yes.

Danny looks down at the bruised face. 'Are you OK?'

No nod from Harry Mangam. His neck is in a brace. He does manage a sound however, a kind of low hiss. That too means yes.

'Does anybody want to accompany him to hospital?' asks the paramedic. 'I can only allow two people.'

'You and your grandmother go,' says Mum. 'I'll follow you down.'

'I'll run you,' says Des.

Danny climbs into the ambulance and holds Gran's hands as it accelerates up Cork Terrace.

'He's going to be all right,' Danny tells her. 'Everything is.'

17

Danny

It is eight o'clock in the evening before they finally get to see Grandad again. The moment they arrived at the hospital he was whisked away on a gurney. Mum and Gran go to talk to the doctor while Danny sits by the old man's bed. Danny doesn't think about him as Grumbleguts any more, just the old man. An old man who has risked everything to fight for his family.

'Maybe I should have gone out for some grapes,' says Danny.

'Couldn't eat them anyway,' mumbles Grandad. He sounds as if he is talking through cotton wool. 'Bet you couldn't either.'

Danny is suddenly aware of his own cuts and bruises. 'This,' he says, gingerly touching his face. 'It's nothing. What about you? Are you going to be all right?'

Grandad goes to nod then grimaces. 'I wish I hadn't done that.'

'Where does it hurt?'

Grandad smiles through a grey mask of a face. 'Everywhere. They got that lunatic, didn't they?'

'Chris? Yes, they got him. We've got you to thank for that, and . . .' Danny hesitates.

'Des. It's OK, son, you can say it. I saw him when I was lying in the hallway. A bit of a turn-up for the book that, me grateful to tha . . . to him.'

172

Danny leans forward. 'He's here, Grandad, at the hospital. You won't make a scene, will you?'

'No lad, Harry Mangam's had enough excitement for one day.'

Just then, Mum and Gran walk into the side room where Danny is talking to his grandfather.

'Go on, what did they say about me?'

Gran smiles. 'Only that you're a tough old boot. You've got a badly bruised collar-bone and a lot of facial swelling. You won't be eating steak for a while. Unless I can liquidise it.'

'Remind me to get rid of that stupid baseball bat,' says Grandad.

'I think the police took it,' says Mum. 'Evidence.'

Danny likes the sound of the word. It calls to mind other words: trial, conviction, justice. That's what he wants for Mum, justice. The end of fear, the beginning of a new life. He lets the word move through his mind like a healing mist.

Justice.

Cathy

She watches as Mum reaches out to hold Dad's hand. It is a scene she never expected to see, affection between her parents. As she sits there, reliving the storm that broke over number one, Cork Terrace, Cathy finds herself smiling. Something ended there this afternoon amidst the litter of glass and plaster. Fifteen years of loneliness and broken dreams. The seed of something was planted too. She can't make out the shape of the flower as yet, she can't feel its texture, see its colours, smell its scent. But she knows it can grow into something beautiful and strong. As beautiful and strong as her son.

She glances at Danny. He has witnessed so much, things no teenage boy should have to experience, but he has come through it all full of pride and hope. He fought today, fought

173

for her. They all did. Most of all she fought for herself and started to put the bad times behind her.

That was the worst really, the way Chris took her over, the way he reduced her to such a state that she made excuses for him, lied about his meanness and cruelty to her own son.

You must have hated me for that, Danny.

'Are you all right, Danny?' she asks.

His brown eyes meet hers. There is no disappointment in them, only trust and love. She has come through with his affection for her intact. 'Yes,' Danny answers. 'I ache a bit, that's all.'

Then something registers in those deep, brown eyes. Recognition. He understands what she really means. Is he OK inside?

'Mum, everything's fine.'

She smiles. 'Yes, I know.'

Danny

Des knocks on the door. Grandad looks up and registers the newcomer, but that's all. Nothing passes between the two men, no looks, no smiles, no words. Fifteen years is a wide, wide canyon and you don't build a bridge across it in a hurry.

'Danny, your girl's here – Nikki.'

Danny puts a hand on Mum's wrist. 'Can I go and see her?'

'Of course you can.'

Danny joins Des outside and does a double take.

'Something the matter?' asks Des.

'Recognise him?'

Des follows the direction in which Danny is looking. There, in the first bed in the room opposite Harry Mangam's is Steve Parker. His jaw is wired up, his eyes dark blue swellings.

'Yes, it's that lad who was giving you aggro the other night.'

'Steve Parker. He was the first to get in Chris's way.'

'I don't think he'll be giving you much trouble for a while.'

Danny smiles. 'No, I don't think he will either. So where's Nikki?'

Des leads the way to the small coffee bar in the foyer. Nikki immediately runs to him and throws her arms round him. 'Thank goodness you're all right.'

Danny feels her tears on his face. 'Hey, there's no need to cry.' He notices Nikki's dad and brother and smiles.

'We'll be in the car, Nik,' says her dad. 'Join us when you're ready.'

'He's all right, your dad,' says Danny. 'Really laid back.'

'Yes, he's great. Is your grandad OK?'

Danny nods. 'He could have got himself killed, though. Chris is . . .' He searches for the right word. 'He's an animal. Speaking of animals, Steve's in there too. Broken jaw. He's all wired up.'

'Good,' says Nikki, 'It might stop him spouting his rubbish.' Her expression changes. 'I was so scared, Danny. Why didn't you tell me about your past?'

Danny shrugs. 'There isn't that much to say. It was bad. We got through it. We ought to be talking about the future.'

'We've got a future then?' asks Nikki.

'You betcha,' says Danny. 'You were great today, Nikki.' He notices an old couple eavesdropping and draws closer. 'You know what?' he whispers. 'My heart turns over every time I look at you.'

Nikki rests her palms on his chest and kisses him. As Danny finally pulls away from the embrace he sees Des smiling. He can't help but smile back.

'I'd better go,' says Nikki. 'I just wanted to be sure you were all right.'

'I've never been better,' says Danny.

He watches Nikki go. The funny thing is, he wasn't just saying that. It's the truth.

Chris

He sits in the cell. They've taken his laces and his belt. As if he's got any intention of topping himself. There's a lot of live for, Chrissie boy. OK, so you'll do time over this, but prison won't break you. It never has before. Very slowly and deliberately he inserts his thumbnail under a flaking scale of paint. He begins to scratch a semi circle, a crude letter C. As the minutes go by he carries on scratching, slowly etching his message into the paintwork, until it reads:

Chris/Cathy – forever.

He draws his knees up to his stomach and examines his handiwork. *Forever.* For a few moments he amuses himself imagining her waiting for him outside the prison gates. When he walks free at the end of his stretch she runs forwards, throwing her arms round his neck, letting herself be swung, round and round . . . round and round . . . then the image breaks up and resolves itself into a few scratched marks on the cell wall.

A lot of water will have to flow under the bridge before he gets his Cathy home.

Forever.

Could it be true, Chrissie, have you found a woman who can take you on and win? He lies back, resting his head on his laced fingers.

No, this isn't the end, Cathy girl. It's just the half-time interval. I can be patient. I'll be back. Believe me, I'll be back. Enjoy your freedom.

Then another image flashes into his mind, maybe years from now, of a freed Chris Kane climbing the hill towards the Edge, walking along Cork Terrace, entering the front door of number one.

Enjoy your freedom . . . while it lasts.

Danny

He sits on the wall round an ornamental flower-bed, looking up at the Edge.

'They won't let him go, will they?' Danny asks Des.

'Shouldn't think so, not for a long time. He broke two of that copper's ribs, I've heard. Not a good idea.'

'So what happens next?' says Danny.

'He goes to court.'

Danny smiles. 'No, I mean to us, me and Mum.'

Des frowns. 'How do you mean?'

'Well, there's nothing to stop us going home.' He looks straight at Des. 'London.'

'Is that what you want?'

Danny shrugs. 'I don't know what I want. It's funny, you know. This is the first time in years me or Mum have had any say over where we go next. This time we're not running from anything. We can make our own minds up.'

Des looks at him. 'You had a good life down there, so your mum says.'

'Yes, it was all right,' says Danny. 'Loads of mates. It was good.'

It's starting to rain, big, heavy drops thudding on the concrete forecourt.

'Nothing to keep you round this dump,' says Des.

Danny shrugs. 'I wouldn't go that far.'

'So you might stay?'

Danny smiles, enjoying watching Des wriggle.

'There's a lot of things we might do.'

18

Danny

It's later, much later. Number one, Cork Terrace, has got back to normal. The door frame has been repaired and a new mortice lock fitted. A double-glazed front window has taken the place of the one that shattered under the impact of the bin that Chris Kane threw with such fury. Harry Mangam's roses are blooming and there are new wind chimes tinkling in the breeze. Steve Parker hasn't touched a single one of them. He's had the wires removed from his jaws but he doesn't say as much as he used to. He is subdued. Just as angry and full of hatred as before, but lacking the spur to do anything about it.

But Danny isn't there, looking out at the wind scouring the Edge. He's in London, on his old stamping ground, talking to Abbie.

'I don't know how to thank you,' says Danny. 'You could have got badly hurt, standing up to Chris like that. You don't know what The Animal is capable of.'

'I think I can imagine,' says Abbie. 'Has he been sent down yet?'

'No,' says Danny. 'Sentencing is next Wednesday.'

Abbie glances at the school gates. 'So what did Dicko say to you?'

'Oh, you know, how good it was to see me again. How glad he was that we could put *that unpleasant business* behind us. After that we just talked about my progress at cross-country.'

'Typical of Dicko,' says Abbie. 'He likes his trophy cabinet to be full. Even if he couldn't waddle round a racetrack to save his life.'

Danny laughs. 'Seriously though, Abbie, you've been one hell of a friend.'

Abbie thumps Danny on the arm. 'Knock it off, will you? I don't want you going all soppy on me. If you want soppy, here's somebody who'll appreciate it.' Ramila is walking towards them.

'I'll be at the paper shop,' says Abbie. 'I'm going to get a can. Come over when you've finished talking to Ramila.'

Danny nods and turns in her direction. 'Hi there.'

'Hi yourself.' She turns her head to one side. 'So who's this Nikki then?'

Danny gives a half-grimace. 'Abbie told you then?'

Ramila nods, giving him a knowing smile. 'Bit of a blonde bombshell, I hear.'

'Listen,' says Danny. 'I never meant it to happen. I mean, I thought I'd never see you again. I didn't mean to play you, or anything . . .'

'Play me?' says Ramila. 'Whatever do you mean?'

'Before I went up north. I was going to ask you out.'

Ramila bursts out laughing. 'You were *what*?'

'I was going to ask you out.'

Ramila purses her lips. 'Tell me you're joking.'

'Not a bit of it,' Danny protests. 'I really fancied you.'

Ramila pulls a face. 'Ye-ew. Danny, you're a mate.'

'You mean you didn't . . . You don't fancy me?'

'Of course not. You're like a brother.' She tosses back her long, black hair. 'Me and you? In that way? Oh no Danny, no.'

Danny stares in disbelief. 'So I read the signs all wrong?' Ramila nods. 'And you're not offended that I'm going out with Nikki?'

'Should I be?'

Danny gives a look of confusion. 'I guess not.'

Abbie is hovering on the pavement opposite, swigging a can of Coke. 'Finished?' he asks.

'Yes,' says Danny. 'Finished.'

Abbie rejoins them. 'So you and this Nikki, you're really serious?'

Danny glances at Ramila, then nods. 'Yes, dead serious.'

'Then we won't hold you up any longer,' says Abbie. 'You'd better get back to your blonde bombshell.'

Danny grins. 'I'm meeting Mum at the station. I'd better be making tracks.'

He starts walking towards the tube. 'Hey, you will keep in touch, won't you?'

'Of course we will,' says Abbie. 'Just as long as you keep that fancy new mobile switched on.'

'Don't worry about that,' says Danny. 'I haven't forgotten since.'

He reaches the tube and looks back. Abbie and Ramila give him a last wave. Danny ducks into the tube and buys his ticket. As he makes his way down to the platform he marvels at how quickly things have changed. This isn't his home any more, just somewhere to visit. Abbie and Ramila are his mates, but he knows that, however much they might want things to be different, they will gradually lose touch. Home is two hundred miles up the railway line, where the winds battle over a long escarpment of rock.

Cathy

She sees Danny striding towards her, swinging his bag.

'Was it difficult?' she asks.

Danny shakes his head. 'No, not really. I've got a new life. They understand that.'

'And you don't mind?'

Danny's face breaks into a smile. 'What's to mind?'

Quite a lot, thinks Cathy. She was so nervous when she put it to him, that they stay on the Edge. Besides Nikki, what was there to keep him there? Steve Parker and his vicious group of young thugs, the small-minded people with their mean, backward ideas, the headteacher who thought the victim was as bad as the bullies, the burned-out shop and its hateful message?

And yet he had agreed readily. Not only that, but in the weeks since Chris's arrest Danny had given every sign of loving his new life. He sat talking to Gran for hours, making the old lady purr with pleasure at the attention. Sometimes he even had time to listen to old Grumbleguts' stories. He was doing well at school too, getting good grades and representing his school in the quiz team and at distance running. Most surprisingly of all, when she had come to him a fortnight ago and asked if he minded her going out for a meal with Des, he had simply smiled and said: 'It's taken the pair of you long enough.'

At the thought of his reaction, Cathy finds herself smiling.

'What's so funny?' asks Danny.

'You,' Cathy tells him.

'Why am I funny?'

Cathy leans forward and strokes his cheek.

'Mu-um,' he protests, simultaneously pulling away and looking round.

'You just are,' she tells him.

Joan

Joan has been sitting watching TV for ten minutes, wondering what's different. Then she realises: I am. She is actually sitting down, enjoying a good film. In an hour Cathy and Danny will be back from London and her family will be home again. My family! Tears start in her eyes at the very thought of it. Fifteen years she has virtually sprinted round the house, busying herself with anything and everything, just so she didn't have to look at Harry, remember how he drove love out of this house. But now she is getting to know him all over again, beginning to rediscover the man who was once her life.

From time to time she wants to scream out loud. All those wasted years. All that time they didn't talk, didn't touch, didn't love. Then she smiles. She has remembered something her own mother used to tell her. When you look at a cup of tea, she would say, don't go grumbling that it's half empty, be happy that it's half full. Well, Joanie love, this cup of yours is more than half full. Since Cathy and Danny came home it's brimming over. Danny's the one who has made all the difference. So alive, so strong. It's as if the three of them have rebuilt their lives on his young shoulders. Joanie smiles imagining Danny getting off the train. She reaches out and takes Harry's hand.

'They'll be home soon,' she says, giving the hand a squeeze.

Harry smiles and squeezes back.

Danny

He puts down his book and looks at Mum. She has her eyes closed. She isn't asleep. How does she put it? Yes, resting her eyes. Danny watches her resting her eyes. The fear lines have gone now. Even the way she sits is different since Chris was finally taken from her life. She is easy with herself and with the world around her. Danny smiles as he remembers how nervous and excited she got about that first date with Des. Like a teenager. But not quite. He knows she won't go rushing into anything. She's stronger now, she's the one who tells Des what's what, not the other way round.

Danny looks out of the window and watches the country-side flashing past.

It's about another hour before they pull in at the tacky little station overlooked by the Edge. Nikki phoned him on his mobile fifteen minutes ago to let him know she would be meeting him on the platform. He imagines her sparkling eyes, her strawberry-blonde hair. He smiles. There you go Abbie, I told you I'd always keep my phone on.

He imagines the lowering mass of the Edge approaching through the late afternoon and feels a rush of exhilaration as powerful as in the last fifty metres of a race.

He's looking forward to it, to freedom, to the promised land.

Shadow of the Minotaur

'Real life' or the death defying adventures of the Greek myths, with their heroes and monsters, daring deeds and narrow escapes – which would you choose?

For Phoenix it's easy. He hates his new home and the new school where he is bullied. He's embarrassed by his computer geek dad. But when he logs on to the Legendeer, the game his dad is working on, he can be a hero. He is Theseus fighting the terrifying Minotaur, or Perseus battling with snake-haired Medusa.

The trouble is The Legendeer is more than just a game. Play it if you dare.

Vampyr Legion

What if there are real worlds where our nightmares live and wait for us?

Phoenix has found one and it's alive. Armies of bloodsucking vampyrs and terrifying werewolves, the creatures of our darkest dreams, are poised to invade our world.

But Phoenix has encountered the creator of *Vampyr Legion*, the evil Gamesmaster, before and knows that this deadly computer game is for real – he must win or never come back.

Warriors of the Raven

The game opens up the gateway between our world and the world of the myths.

The Gamesmaster almost has our world at his mercy. Twice before fourteen-year-old Phoenix has battled against him in *Shadow of the Minotaur* and *Vampyr Legion*, but Warriors of the Raven is the game at its most complex and deadly level. This time, Phoenix enters the arena for the final conflict, set in the world of Norse myth. Join Phoenix in Asgard to fight Loki, the Mischief-maker, the terrifying Valkyries, dragons and fire demons – and hope for victory. Our future depends on him.

Chicken

'All I could think about was Webbo and what he had in store for me.'

Davy's too chicken to stand up to bullying at school. He's been singled out as an easy target. His family aren't much help – they're all chicken too. Mum's frightened of learning to drive, big brother Col is terrifying himself trying to impress his new friends. And Dad has too many problems of his own to be sympathetic.

But in the end it's his little sister's strange secret which spurs Davy on . . . and surprises the whole family as well.

Ganging Up

John and Gerry have always been friends, brought together by their passion for football. Then Gerry's dad loses his job and everything turns sour. The two boys had always steered clear of the gangs at school, but Gerry gets drawn in and now he and John find themselves standing on opposite sides.

Set in a tough inner city Liverpool estate, this is a story about friendships, rivalries and survival played out at school and on the football field.

Whose Side Are You On

SOME THINGS ARE WORTH FIGHTING FOR . . .

Mattie likes a quiet life. When the school bullies start picking on his Asian friend, Pravin, he knows he should do something about it. Too scared to act, Mattie runs away. But instead of escaping, somehow he is transported to the very heart of slavery, a sugar plantation in eighteenth-century Jamaica, not knowing whether he will return home . . .